Our Hollow Sofa

Cynthia Rowe

First published August 2004

National Library of Australia Cataloguing-in-Publication Data

Rowe, Cynthia. Our hollow sofa.

ISBN: 0987455400

ISBN 13: 978-0-9874554-0-6

I. Title.

A823.4

By the same author:

Ants in My Dreadlocks

Stinger in a Sugar Jar

My French Barrette

Couscous Threads

Bad Grass

Driftwood – poetry collection

About the Author

Cynthia Rowe has a degree from the University of Melbourne and has taught French and English for most of her working life. She has also spent time in France and the French Territories and was awarded a *Diplôme Approfondi de Langue Française* by the French Ministry of Education. She is a Writing Fellow of the Fellowship of Australian Writers NSW.

Cynthia's short stories have appeared in magazines and been broadcast on National Community Radio. Her poetry has won many awards and can be read in numerous literary journals internationally. She is Editor: Haiku Xpressions; President: Australian Haiku Society; Past President: Eastern Suburbs Branch (Bondi Writers) Fellowship of Australian Writers NSW.

Our Hollow Sofa is her first book in the Genna Perrier series.

For Bruce

Acknowledgements

My thanks go to Belinda and her ZenithOptimedia team; Simon for his computer savvy and Anne Françoise for her insight into life in the French colonies; Scott Cuthbert for advising me on the types of boats and motor vehicles likely to be used in a seaside town.

Sheena Cuthbert's input on student book preferences was invaluable.

I would also like to thank Anna Carmody for her wise editorial comments, and the Waverley Library staff for their support.

As always I am indebted to my husband Bruce and his unfailing encouragement.

Prologue

Our hollow sofa, thinly padded on top, a coffin shape inside, was one of the things that led me to be standing there watching Marcel drive away.

"Sorry, is raining frogs and cats," he'd said, as he let me out beside the slurp of gutter water.

The air had a foggy feel, thick, as if you could cut it into chunks and eat it. Brake lights flared through the drenching wet as his car turned right onto the road leading from the airport. Boy, had *I* been led up, down and around the garden path. Why had I bothered to come?

The sliding doors hissed open. I could see posters of hectic reef fish, ochre dot paintings, skinny waterfalls, crocodiles that made your skin itch to look at them. I should've been glad to be heading home, but my mind swirled with disappointment. A ghetto blaster thumped: *It's got to be-e-e per-fect*. Rumble and squeak of trolley wheels in the delineated aisle of tape.

I hefted my backpack and followed the tumbrel sound. The guy with the mullet took his boarding pass. The check-in chick nodded in my direction. I sidled up and pointed to the print-out.

"There's a ticket booked for me. Mr Manet said to show this."

"Identity?" Her mouth was pursed, her hair the colour of squashed Chilean bugs.

I jiggled my bus concession out of my pocket, waved it in her direction.

"No, Ms. Perrier," she snapped, eyes hard. "With photo."

"I so *totally* don't have one with photo."

"Driving licence?"

"Don't drive."

"Passport?"

I shook my head.

"How do I know you're you?" She looked at me coldly.

"Of course I'm me!" My eyes frisked the ceiling.

"I need photo ID. That ticket was purchased electronically." With a flick of the shoulder, she nodded to the person behind me in the queue.

"I don't *have* photo ID."

My body was turning into melted jelly in the mugginess and I was beginning to panic. How would I get all the way back to Ravella? I should never have been so screwed up about my birth mother, should've let it rest until I turned eighteen. But eighteen seemed forever away.

My brain began to fizz. "You shlep!" I yelled at the check-in chick, now filing her nails with an emery board.

She nodded her head towards the security man in the knife-pleated shorts. He strutted towards me, knees splayed out as he walked. Who did he think *he* was? The Incredible Hulk? Master Interrogator?

"Do I have to radio the police, Miss?"

"Why? I never said anything about a bomb."

"You just did."

"But I, like, never actually mentioned the word 'bomb'."

"You did again."

Wrong!! As in wrong answer.

"*Zut!*" I said.

"Indecent language. Two offences now."

"*Zut* means *bother* in French, no big deal." I gazed into his fish eyes. This guy wouldn't know a sense of humour if it jumped up and bit him. "I'll behave, whatever." I plonked myself down on a modulated seat. "*Les hommes, je vous en veux,*" I muttered, still stuck in exam mode like a busted CD.

The security man moved off. I hoped he wasn't a linguist with sharp hearing. Anyway, I did hate men. I was *so* over Marcel Manet and this sitch he'd got me into—that DNA test must've been gammon.

The proprietor of the Amedée Apartments in the out-there outfit hadn't been impressed. And I was like, "*Well, sorreee.*" Was it the daggy French plait with the bits of hair bursting from the braid that turned her off? Nope, more like the frizzy fringe created by the hairdresser on the highway. I'd felt like a lard.

Perhaps my birth mother really *was* six feet under? Or was it word play on Namilly's part: forget about your mother, she's no longer here? As, *in your life.*

All other avenues of searching for my origins had drawn blanks. "Try in a few months, when you've come of age," had been the pompous response from the local adoption agencies. Amnesty International sent me off with a flea in my ear. So I lapsed into a sort of suspended activity—apart from those seductive websites, those yummy, chummy chat rooms.

I thought I'd lucked out when Marcel turned up, spun his mouthwatering story, said my birth mother was out there waiting for me to knock on her door.

Yeah, right.

"Look too young to be flying around the country on your own." The security man in the upright walk socks was back.

"Old enough to be married." I stuck out my chest in its best stretch T-shirt.

"Show us your ID then."

"Don't have any dorky ID."

I gazed at the ominous patch of sweat spreading across his chest from his armpits. Beyond the airport, streetlights glowed. Soon the sky would be as thick and black as my mood.

The last of the travellers had disappeared through the departure gates and I could hear the whine of the engines as they revved up for the last flight south. I levered myself off the seat, and wandered to the ladies loo. The first cubicle was grungy. The second a heap of damp tissue. The third? I dragged at the Ferris wheel dispenser, created a clean cover, and lowered myself.

Carn Cairns! said the graffiti on the back of the door. Glad somebody dug living in this ginormous steam bath.

I pulled the photo Marcel had taken of me on the beach from my pocket. A long way, and only this to show for it. What a whopper error leaving my details on those websites. I'd been making lots of whopper errors lately. And letting Marcel lead me on this crazy chase was top of the list.

The woman in the retro pareo had said: *I am not your birth mother*, or words to that effect, with a don't-you-come-around-upsetting-my-lifestyle look on her face.

I felt a void opening up inside of me, knew the sense of hopeful possibility would follow: is this my birth mother, is that my dad? A sort of game I played.

Chapter 1

November 2nd

I fell in the door, hot and sweaty from my English exam. Three Bic pens had melted from the heat thrown by the sun through the plate glass windows of Ravella Community Hall. My writing had turned to barbed wire and spiders by the end. I was frazzled.

I flicked on the TV. Axel Bauer was belting out 'Cargo' on the box. Magic in my head? No way. Just facts, facts, facts and more facts. I bopped my way to the kitchen to grind out a sustaining non-genetically-modified carrot juice.

There were two kitchens in our Ravella home: the sunroom kitchen, and my kitchen. Namilly, knocked back for a loan to renovate her culinary area, had moved her cooking utensils into a room facing south called 'the sunroom'. Denied the right to relocate to the sunless sunroom, she intended to cook there just the same. So she sat like a broody hen, hunched over her electric frypan as the fumes funnelled towards the ceiling. They deposited a layer of thick yellow grease across the plasterboard. The sight of it had sent me spiralling into a raw vegan regime.

Big on mystery burgers, Namilly'd made me see the light. I followed the fresh food trail whenever I stocked up at The Store—better for the health and even better for the brain when left uncooked. Namilly, on the other hand, had a thing for canned foods, particularly of the bean variety. All heated through with oceans of extra virgin olive oil. We only had one bathroom—despite the two kitchens—and she scuttled in and out of that pea-green room on a regular basis, leaving the fan grinding and sucking behind her.

I pulled out the juicer, jammed the parts together, shrugged on my waxed apron, and donned my goggles—plastic disposable from the dentist. The machine, stained with age, could put out the eye of anyone who stood up close. I never turned it on without my safety specs.

The pieces of carrot bounded and jumped. The engine groaned. Golden-red juice oozed and dribbled from the spout into the jug with rabbits etched along the side. A gale of carrot dust spewed across my face and arms. A chunk of the vegetable bounced upwards, making for the hood of the extractor fan.

I did a nifty overhead smash. (The Ravella High tennis team, consisting of Fat Betty, Angela, Hetty and myself, had bombed in the comp that year—I blamed it on Hetty's oversized nerd glasses, she blamed it on Fat Betty's oversized legs.) After swatting the carrot cube back into the spout, I swigged the foamy liquid in one gulp without bothering to decant into a tumbler.

That was my vision dealt with. Next I needed brain food—the dinky-di stuff.

Unable to think of any vegetable that might do the trick, I stretched my hand deep into the shadowy recesses of the corner cupboard. Bingo. My decrepit can of sardines was still there.

I hauled on the ring pull, and prodded the tightly packed soldiers. Apart from a bit of brown poo around the edges, they looked perfectly fine to me.

As each small fish glided down my throat on a river of silken oil, I could feel it doing me good. My brains were burgeoning, my body surging. I felt a lump in my throat. My chest contracted. I ran. I flung open the door of the bathroom, and retched into the toilet. Blearing into the bowl, I boggled. Was that a whole sardine glaring at me in the water?

"Ugh, gross." I flushed it off on its journey to the septic tank, and trailed back to the kitchen. Namilly, disappearing most afternoons lately, was always banging on about my eating habits. "You must've been a projectile vomiter," she'd say, as if my past was a mystery to her.

I was skinny as a piece of string and olive-skinned. She said I was a Caldoche, born in Noumea during the terrible Events, and I wanted to believe her. It gave me something to hang on to, a feeling of identity. But she was sketchy on the details whenever I brought the subject up.

I inspected a vine-ripened tomato with a bruise on one side. Contemplating whether to risk eating it, I heard a voice say, "How'd the exam go, Genna?"

I turned. Win Winstone stood in the doorway, jeans neatly pressed— the only person in the universe who pressed her jeans. Ice-blonde hair flowed down the back of her Bamboo T-shirt.

"Boring as bat droppings." I muttered.

"Well, the ritual and shebang is not devised for your entertainment." Win wandered to the kitchen window. She peered through the glass, smeary with the salt air. "Is that Stefan Becker standing on the other side of the gate?"

I gazed over her shoulder. "Sure is."

"What's he doing? He looks space age nerdy."

"Waiting for me to come out."

"Why doesn't he come in, knock on the door?"

"Namilly, he's scared witless of her."

"Still, after all these years? How odd." Win screwed up her nose.

"You seen Namilly? She's gone again, been disappearing a lot lately," I said.

Win shrugged. "Your mum still chucking her empties over the fence, Gen? Stink's somethin' terrible."

She was right. Namilly hurled her empty cans over the fence into the scrubby land next door. They sailed through the air, food spray streaming behind like surplus rocket fuel. They clinked against the pile, rattled and settled. The flies gorged themselves until the rains came and washed the metal clean. On warm days, the miasma from the block next door was scarily festy.

"Can I boot up, use your cyberspace?" Win's violet eyes veered away from mine. I knew which sites *she* planned to surf. (Win was a mouse potato, and mostly on my computer.)

"Yours still on the blink? Been a long time since it needed fixing."

She fiddled with her plain gold ear stud—Win used to be a Tac Tac girl with a row of silver hoops along the helix. "Yeah, I know. It's 'cause of Ma. She's still sauntering around on the other side of the globe."

Win's lips flapped as she talked, as if she had something important to tell me about her mother. As if she couldn't bring herself to spit it out.

"Could be hard to see, the screen's developed this water feature."

Win raised a finely plucked eyebrow. "Water feature?"

"Mmm. Like a fish shop window. Nah, more like corrugated iron in a rainstorm." I knew because I'd been investigating adoption sites: *birthmother.com*, *babesinwoods. com*. Lately, I'd become a net chick.

"Think I'll leave it." As Win peered through the window again, I smelled ammonia on her T-shirt. "Stef's still outside the gate. You gonna invite him in, go hunt blue ringers, whatever it is you do with him? Dunno how you can *stand* to get close to those crimson zits."

"He's my mate," I said, feeling my mouth turn into a squinchy line.

She turned to go, and I noticed Win's breath was sweet. Gardenias? Musky rose? Whatever—it clashed with the pee smell on her T-shirt. Win was no dopehead. Like me, she only smoked the odd chop-chop rollie—illegal tobacco, but good for the health if you ignored the bleach, the mould, the bits of sticky straw used for padding.

"Cool, if he turns you on." She sloped towards the back door, stopped, said over her shoulder, "You've got an orange upper lip, Gen."

I ran the back of my hand across my mouth, wiping away the carrot moustache and wondering about Win's breath. Had she developed diabetes?

I watched her go, asking myself, *How come she swanned in and out of my pad as if she owned it, when she never put out the welcome mat for me?*

Win and I never spoke about her family. That was bug-off stuff. Anyway, not the nitty-gritty one whispers about with a buddy. I was never her come-into-my-home friend, only her goodbye-at-the-gate friend. Win was a loner, and I often wondered why. I'd glimpsed her mother from time to time, but not lately. Alice Winstone was always away on business. Win said she was editor of an up-market fashion magazine—yeah, a bit like Vogue.

I remembered Alice as being a foxy lady. Although her hair was frequently tousled and her speech tended to be slurred. Win's father? Kingsley Winstone worked in China, a diplomat or something. I was sure her parents were divorced. If not, Kingsley Winstone was a permanently absent father.

I peered out the kitchen window. Stefan stood there still, a jar in his hand. I threw up the sash.

"See ya on the rocks, mate."

"Should be a good crop, unless the wind picks up!" he called.

He marched off, all zinc cream and business. His hair glinted in the sun. His face was a mask of white protection. He resembled an alien from *X-Files*.

My friendship with Stefan was blokey rather than dreamy. He was a friend-friend, although lately I'd detected a gleam of something more in his eyes.

Win thought we were having it off. But she was wrong. I hadn't had it off with anybody yet. All Stef and I did was hunt blue ringers, a death-defying occupation. We'd been doing it for years. (Perhaps Stefan, a blue ringer collector, hoped I'd be stung. Then mouth-to-mouth for twenty-four hours. *As if!*) We'd poke the shy medusa with a stick, and watch it turn from pallid to lurid until its rings glowed. Watch it writhe with fury, flare fluorescent, spit venom in our direction. Then we'd cling and giggle, prance from rock to rock, pretend to be over the moon with terror.

Sometimes he'd catch one. Stefan kept rows and rows of jars in his bedroom, tiny octopuses hanging upside down like limp rags behind the glass.

Where were we headed after our blue ringer phase? His sunburn and zits were too off-putting, so it was mind-boggling to think of anything more than a cuz handhold, a bro arm around the shoulder. But we'd come a long way since he flicked bogeys at me in primary school.

Stefan and I didn't *go* out together. We *hung* out together. And I could talk to him about almost anything. No SNAG, low on the eye candy chain, Stefan Becker was my soul mate.

Chapter 2

I pulled the juicer apart, ran hot water with a dash of detergent into the sink.

As I dumped the lot to soak a cockroach scooted past, and squeezed beneath the kickboard of the cupboard—probably a refugee from Namilly's sunroom kitchen. Yikes! I needed to buy a bomb, prevent the cockie from creeping into my ear at night. (A disaster for any oral exam.)

Darting into the living room, I hefted my worn backpack—for which I'd paid Angela Rasmussen $7.55, plus a loan of my copy of *Merde! The French Your Teachers Never Taught You*—from the floor onto Namilly's hollow sofa. Angela, impressed by the mind-blowing array of swear words inside the thumbed pages, was probably practising them on Jason Bjorkman, her current hot date, right now.

I picked up a melted Bic from the floor, tucked it back into the backpack and briefly considered heaving the bag into my room. (I knew Namilly fossicked among my things.)

Poking my finger through the gap in the canvas, I retrieved the pen, and placed it strategically on top. Memorised the spot.

I almost knocked Namilly over as I flew out the door to meet Stefan. She barely acknowledged my existence, which was not unusual. We never watched movies together, or did mumsie things. What *was* unusual was the antiseptic smell of her clothing, the underlying pong of ammonia—nothing like the stink of empty cans stewing on the other side of the fence. No, this was a hospital whiff.

I screeched to a halt. *Win had smelled like that, too.* Apart from her floral breath. Why did everyone smell pissy and odd lately?

Despite her lined face, I didn't think Namilly'd reached *that* stage of her life. Her ESR was elevated, her cholesterol was up—she made a loaf for that, a gluggy log of cooked oatmeal. Oh, and her hot flushes had started. No, something else was going on, something to do with her disappearances.

I didn't have time to quiz her. Stefan was waiting.

I jogged past Grassberger's Guesthouse, known as Last Gasp Guesthouse due to the imminent use-by date of its residents, to the top of the cliff. I swerved onto the track leading to the beach. Hugging my arms to my body, I skidded down the sandy loam. The wind, straight off the Antarctic, had picked up. It stirred the waters of the Bay into neat waves that hissed and swirled onto the coarse-grained sand.

The spiky dune grass snatched at my legs as I hurried past the spot where Namilly'd hacked off the end of my toe with my new beach shovel at the age of six. The scar was still there to taunt me. And I often wondered if she'd done it on purpose.

Namilly hated the beach. It was the last time she ever went there. After that, I became a serial hanger-on, tagging along with anybody headed in the direction of any sort of water.

A lizard twitched its tongue at me.

Whispers and giggles came from the bleached blue bathing box at the end of the path, the paint-blistered one belonging to the Rasmussen family. I could hear the words '*Baise-moi*' repeated over and over.

I felt my face flush. Was Angela putting those French words into practice? Celebrating the end of her first exam with Jason?

Angela, world famous backscratcher, with springy hair and apple cheeks, was the ace nympho of Ravella High. She'd been through them all. Deck from the Bottle Shop. Zac with the pecs and the spray-on pants. A bloke they called Hank With Attitude, and spoke about in hushed whispers.

Angela was out there.

Her current boyfriend was nice Jason, with his Armani jeans and triple-pierced tongue. Year 12 under her belt, I could see she was aiming for a meringue wedding dress.

The tide had heaped the sand into ridged piles. Stefan was on the rocks, bent over, prodding around with a piece of driftwood. The house on Ti Point towered above. The pine trees surrounding it slew wispy taunts at the rococo dwelling.

"Find any?" I yelled.

Stefan straightened. He pointed at the empty Vegemite jar. His smile was yellow against the white of the zinc cream. The insides of his ears were almost translucent. His fingernails were chewed right down from the tension of writing an essay about the effect of Islam on the life of Betty Mahmoody. (It hadn't been easy for me, either. Namilly, bilingual and a voracious reader, had refused to fork out for a copy of the book in English. So I struggled all year with *Jamais sans ma fille*, translating frantically as we ploughed our way through the text.)

"You're not planning to catch one in that thing?" I squeaked, freaking at the smallness of the jar.

"Thought I might."

"Be suicide, mate."

"Not a bad way to go. Get away from the torture I'm goin' through. Whole thing sucks, geared for girls."

"There was a choice, Stef. You could've wrestled with Albert Camus."

"I only like *The Caine Mutiny*, read it five times."

"That's *ferocious*. You and Captain Queeg must be best mates by now." Seeing him scowl, I decided to change the subject to one closer to his heart. "Any blue ringers?"

"Nah, wind's too strong. Too hard to see the buggers."

"Let's go round to The Cauldron. Might be one or two thrown up with the waves, hiding in a Coke can or something."

"Nah, day's too rough."

"C'mon, it'll be grouse."

I was tugging on Stefan's Boomdogger top when I saw a stranger picking his way across the rocks. He was dressed in the European style—baggy and chichi. He stopped, turned, looked out to sea.

For a brief moment I wondered if it was Kingsley Winstone, back from China to see Win. But this was no stodgy, stitched-up business-man. His hair was thin, but no sign of grey. He was sophisticated, flash. With his lightweight linen trousers, he wore a long-sleeved shirt. A dark sweater was slung across his shoulders. His feet were clad in navy-blue boat shoes, new looking, not a speck of dirt upon them, not one gap in the canvas. This man was definitely not a local.

"Comin', mate?" Stefan interrupted my thoughts. "Or too busy perving?"

"Get real. He's old enough to be my," I murmured, scratching my head, "father."

The word 'father' reminded me of that other missing chunk in my life.

Was this stranger staying in the house on Ti Point? The house had been unoccupied for months, with strips of paint hanging from its rose-covered walls. The mullioned windows were smeary with the spray thrown up from the waves thrusting onto the rocks below. The Cauldron churned nearby, that part of the sea that surged and swelled on the finest day over Selwyn's Fault—a fault line on the sea floor—when the rest of Port Phillip Bay was flat as a millpond.

The pines pitched. The wind howled. The sound was eerie and keening.

The stranger was deep in thought. He lifted his hip shades from his forehead, jammed them onto his nose and began to negotiate the boul-ders. Wearily, he climbed the steps hewn into the side of the cliff. What did *he* have to be weary about, dressed in groovy gear like that? With gear like that, I'd be spinning like a top with happiness.

I followed Stefan, staring.

A pain shot through my Namilly-scarred toe. The blue-ringer jar, slipped from Stefan's grasp, glanced off my foot and shattered into pieces.

"*Merde!*" I leaned down to inspect the damage.

The foreigner stopped. He hesitated, as if about to come back down, maybe say something. He changed his mind, and continued on until he was swallowed up by the splintered gate.

Was this cool dude in Ravella for long? I wondered. Or simply pass-ing through? Like me, he didn't have that Anglo-Celtic look. I longed to meet him.

"S'matter?" Stefan was gazing at me.

"Nothing."

"That time of the month?"

"What do *you* know about *that time of the month*?"

"Skye gets peed off easily when those four weeks, like, *roll* around. And they career up with regulous monotony."

"You mean monotonous regularity. Anyway, don't compare *me* to your ditsy older sister," I snapped.

Stefan was wrong. It was the sardines. I should've stuck to my raw vegan diet, at least until the exams were over.

"Sorry, gotta go."

I could see Elizabeth Stubbs, serious contender for Stefan's affections, skulking in her gold-flecked jellies near the bushes at the top of the cliff. Her basin-cut hair fluttered in the breeze like the flags on Vince Becker's service station driveway.

"Fat Betty's waiting," I said.

"You mean Elizabeth." Stefan looked as though he'd gulped down a whole bowl of blue ringers. His ears had gone pale in the wind. His zinc cream face pack was melting like ice shavings on a hot summer's day. Would he turn into a puddle if I stayed?

"Well, pardon me for wasting space, but her legs alone weigh more than *I* do!"

I ploughed my way back along the sand. I had stacks to do. Revision for vegie maths. The purchase of a cockroach bomb. The row of topiary box plants on my windowsill to be clipped and watered—sort of like caring for a poodle (Namilly's idea, to strengthen my moral fibre). And I'd met a new chum in the chat room, got to know him well enough to stop using those yucky fake names. Gem, Jam, Juice.

"Hi, I'm Genna," I'd said, up-front for the first time.

Jules and I were due to meet in cyberspace that night, to talk about our origins. Same age as me, he sounded spunky.

I clambered up the track. Fat Betty—pizza aficionado and droob— had disappeared from the cliff top. Was I jealous of Elizabeth? As if. No one could find Stefan's facial happenings attractive. And did he find her tree-trunk legs a turn-on?

I tried to like Elizabeth Stubbs. Really. Even when she let that lob drop into the court on match point against Eastern Lakes High. "It's okay," I'd said. But she looked at me in that personality-free-zone way of hers. And somehow I felt guilty.

I began to think of Angela again, having it off while I was left with her ratty backpack. A thought struck me: *Jason's face was smooth as the proverbial baby's bottom.* Were babes and zits mutually exclusive? If so, would I help out Stefan in the cause of medical intervention? Nope, I decided, that'd be stretching mateship too far.

My mind scrabbled with an idea. Would Jules, my chat room pal, be the answer to my boyfriend problems?

Angela claimed it was the fake Jimmy Choo shoes she bought in Kingston—a short bus ride from Ravella—that made her sick on legs. Deep down, I knew it was my French book.

Chapter 3

I darted into the house for money and to check the messages on my voicemail, discover if the Department of Human Services had returned my call regarding my birth mother. (Although, if Namilly was telling the truth, she was six feet under, buried in a grave beneath foreign swaying palms.)

Before checking my messages, I dashed into the living room to extract some dough from my backpack—that cockroach bomb was imperative. I would also see if the melted Bic had been moved, see if Namilly'd been fossicking among my things.

The whole kit and caboodle confronted me in a spray of possessions. Three Bics in an inky puddle of red and black. Dog-eared books heaped at odd angles. Sheets of paper scattered about like abandoned floor tiles. My last minute list of multi-functional quotations, suitable for insertion in any examinable subject. Bus concessions—one expired, one current. An old chop-chop rollie pulled apart and sprinkled like fibrous snow.

Namilly hadn't attempted to be subtle in her search.

The contents of a packet of Minties had been tossed everywhere, the sweets untwisted and all over the place, as if she'd examined them. Did she think I kept illegal substances wrapped up in Mintie papers?

The lid of our hollow sofa—upholstered in a zigzag pattern with the occasional interspersed flower—was thrown back against the wall. And Namilly sat before it.

She was ranging cans of different shapes and sizes in pairs and lines and circles. All were being placed in some kind of oblique order. She slowly pushed with one finger. Her signet ring, no coat of arms inscribed, gleamed dully. The floor resembled a giant Ouija board, using objects instead of letters of the alphabet. Was this some New Age bizzo involving canned foods?

"Hellooo," I shouted in her ear, cranky that she'd invaded my privacy. She didn't answer.

She continued to sit there talking to herself. She pushed her cans this way and that, breaking ranks from rigid lines. Creating new grid patterns. Forming circles as if to protect the wagons, the sheriff and the horses. A can of pickled pork stood in the middle like a watchtower. A whiff of antiseptic upon her, she was bent over, murmuring in a mishmash of French and English.

Her hair was like a thicket of troubled thoughts.

"My things, you've been touching my things!" The telephone buzzed. "Hello." I jammed the receiver against my ear.

"Tenants Union here."

"Who?"

"Tenants Union, you were making inquiries?"

"Nooo, it was about—"

"'Fraid you'll have to go to the Tribunal. VCAT specifies it. But not if you're a legal person."

"Legal person?"

"Lawyer, they're banned." The man at the other end sounded tired.

"But I was inquiring about adoption. What's this to do—?"

"Dunno, young lady. Human Services handballed your case on to me. Just bring your RTA with you, plus any other papers."

"RTA?"

"Residential Tenancy Agreement."

"But," I spluttered. "Oh, forget it."

Namilly continued to play calmly with her cans, as if she'd not heard the 'adoption' word. As if she'd never heard the call at all. And I didn't have time to find out what was bugging her.

Sunshine dazzled on a tin of ham, sent shock waves flashing through my mind. What if Namilly'd never formally adopted me? It wasn't easy to adopt if you were single.

I stuffed the money for the bomb in my pocket. I knew just the place to get it. The Zabaglione Woollen Shop. As long as Mrs Bradfield's husband, dirty-old-creep Jack, wasn't hanging about perving.

Chapter 4

I plucked two banana passionfruits from the vine straggling over our house. Jammed one into my pocket. Splitting the other open with my thumbnail, I pushed my tongue inside, curled it upward and scooped the fruit from the cleft. Namilly's banana passionfruits were to die for.

The flies buzzed on the other side of the brush fence, gorging on her latest offering as I yanked open the cyclone gate and headed for the highway, the hub of our fresh air town.

Roads in Ravella curved in wide, looping circles. Getting from A to B could take forever. So I sheared off Ravella Crescent, plunging into the ti-tree bushes on my way to the Zabaglione Woollen Shop. (A haberdashery knick-knack place, it'd been an Italian restaurant in a former life.) Namilly's friend, Mrs B, was the whispery proprietor. She sold the most amazing cockroach bombs in plain grey wrappers. You could turn feral from the fumes, but the cockies turned belly up in no time flat.

The cowbell jangled as I burst through the glass door. The shop was dysfunctional, as if the owner had a problem. And, according to the locals, that problem was Jack.

Blown glass animals nudged music boxes carved with Astérix characters. Chaotic skeins of wool. Sanitary napkins mixed with baby bibs. Frilly shirts that were so last millennium.

An unused espresso machine sat to one side on a bench. Next to it, four hand-made cardigans dripped with naff bobbles. A sign: Namilly's Knitteds. The shop smelled of camphor.

Mrs B was famous for her chop-chop. It sat beneath the counter, and she flogged it to the students of Ravella High on a regular basis, no questions asked. Chop-chop was cheaper to buy than regular rolling tobacco and Mrs B did a roaring trade, doling it out in dinky little paper bags.

Hetty Geiger—study-head friend, bad tennis player and classmate—was a *big* chop-chop smoker. She did it for health reasons, she said, purer and safer than ordinary tobacco. According to Hetty, chop-chop was free of nicotine. But, apart from the odd rollie, I never smoked it much at all. And neither did Win.

Mrs B, copper half-bangle on her wrist, drifted through from the back of the shop. A full-sized matching bangle was wrapped around her flag arm, perched above the elbow, from which hung a lace hanky. She spent her time wiping her nose with it, carefully, before tucking the hanky back beneath the bangle.

A fat Jack Russell sniffled on the floor behind the counter. The other Jack, her better half and the town Peeping Tom, was nowhere to be seen. (Like any good serial voyeur, he was mostly seen at night. And always by Hetty Geiger, who said he climbed through her bedroom window on a regular basis—just to look.)

I pulled my money from beneath the spare banana passionfruit. "Grey bomb, please." I waved the ten dollars.

I could see no bombs on the counter. Were they hidden below with the chop-chop?

"Sorry, dearie. Sold the last two minutes ago." Mrs B looked disappointed.

"What'll I do? I'm desperate. It's my ears, my oral exam, they could get in!"

"Try the opposition, dearie." She hiccuped, and gave me a sly smile.

I locked eyeballs with her. Had Mrs B been smoking her own chop-chop? If so, had the latest batch been cut with mushroom-impregnated straw?

As I emerged into the afternoon light, an idea occurred to me: had Namilly had a heart-to-heart about my origins with Mrs B, discussed my birth mother? I turned back. The hand-written sign read Closed.

I cupped my hands, and peered through the glass. Jack was with her. The two of them were arguing.

I crossed the road. The aisles of The Store were jammed with kids gorging on loose nuts and dried fruit. I grabbed a commercially manufactured bomb from the shelf and headed for the checkout.

Chapter 5

I decided to take the short cut back, ramble through the ti-tree bushes. Chill out from my studies before the sun became a low ball and disappeared.

I slung the plastic bag over my shoulder, unable to stop thinking about the man on Ti Point. Why was he in Ravella? And would I ever get to meet him?

My mind swirled. Was this person simply Win's father, back home for a break? Unlikely. He'd looked way too European.

I began to ponder about Win. She was detached these days, as if she knew something I did not. With her bodacious ice-blonde hair, she made me feel inferior. At times, I was grateful she deigned to talk to me.

A sound intruded on my thoughts. A rustle. A twig snapped, and I ground to a halt. A brush fowl? They often pecked and scratched in the undergrowth late in the day.

A snigger.

I froze. Birds didn't snigger. Was it Jack Bradfield? Had he seen me leave the Zabaglione Woollen Shop, and followed me? Would he *do* something? Like throw me to the ground, ravage me? (Then again, Hetty'd said he only looked.)

Should I run, flee while the going was good? No, it'd look crass, dumb. Anyway, I could easily outrun a seventy-year-old codger. Hey,

I was getting my brain in a twist over nothing. On the other hand, men who drooled at young women usually didn't snigger.

A cough. A giggle. My stalker had company, and Jack Bradfield never acted in consort. Were some local kids trying to scare the pants off me?

Another twig snapped.

I smelled the sour smell of sweat, sensed bodies jostling, and turned. My surprise shifted to wariness. Two bogans, older than me, stood there smirking.

They backed off, and began to fade into the scrub. Their black T-shirts were crusty with age. A packet of fags was stuffed beneath a sleeve alongside a snake tattoo. Jeans hung low. Grotty thongs slithered in the dirt.

I gave them a withering look but could feel my heart banging beneath my T-shirt. *I never should've taken that short cut,* I told myself. I should've walked home along Ravella Crescent in view of passing cars. You could get lost in here, too. I knew no one would hear me.

I quickened my step. The bogans quickened theirs.

I broke into a gentle trot. They broke into a gentle trot.

I eased into a slow lope. They eased into a slow lope.

They sniggered. They snorted. They shoved one another. I picked up pace. I dodged through the bushes like a maniac. The cockroach bomb bashed against my side, swinging back and forth like a metronome, reminding me I was in danger.

"Get lost, you mongrels," I panted. "Who do you think you are?"

"Friend of a friend," they chorused.

Friend of a friend? Stefan? (Not his type.) Win? (No boyfriend that I knew of.) Angela? (She was an item with Jason.) Fat Betty? (Forget it. She only hung around Stefan.)

Pounding feet thrummed. I could feel them closing in.

I darted down narrow trails I'd never even seen before. They darted behind me, seeming to know the ti-tree tracks better than I did. They were gaining.

I pounded harder.

Soon I seemed to be running on the spot in a bad dream. Their breathing was heavy. Their bodies were close. They cursed as branches tore at their limbs.

Friend? A friend of a friend? Some friend! I knew of no one who'd spend a nanosecond with nevilles like these.

A pain shot through my ankle. I glanced down briefly. The wayward stick caused me to slow. They edged closer.

Sweat poured into my eyes. Everything stung, became a blur. Hair, car-wash wet, flicked back and forth across my vision. Unable to see, I was losing my sense of direction. The sun had been behind me before. Now it was burning my face.

A branch reached out, snatched at my clothes. Scratched my arms. Whipped against my skin. But there was no pain, only evil-smelling terror.

I felt their breath on my back. I smelled their sweaty nearness. I saw the blur of their oily clothes, heard the drumming of their feet. A hand touched me, lunged for my T-shirt. Grasped me like a ti-tree branch. My legs were on the point of collapsing.

Next thing I knew, the ground had slammed into my face. A vice-like grip on my foot. Loose soil against my lips. I struggled. I grunted. I tried to shake off that hand. I kicked. I kicked again. I kicked until I could kick no longer.

They had me.

My heart hammered. Would they kill me when they were done? Was this how it would all end, in the Ravella dirt? I would never find out about my origins. How dare they take that away from me?

My eyes were tight shut when they flipped me over like a chop on a barbecue. I refused to look. Seeing closed lids, would they let me go when they'd finished? Feel safe? Believe I was unable to identify them?

I got a squidgy, sinking feeling. Who was I kidding? We had spoken. Of *course* I was able to identify them.

"Grab 'er 'ands," one of them panted.

I tasted dry dirt and burnt leaves.

Could I outfox them, outthink their mean little minds? If I kept still they might relax, become cocky. Then, like a gazelle, I could spring away.

The pressure of the hand became softer. A zip sound ripped through my mind. This was it. This was my last chance. I arched, lurched upwards, thrust my pelvis, pushed against the ground, ready to spring. I was too slow. He grabbed me.

"She a bloke? I'm not into that, mate." (Aha, the banana passionfruit was bulging in my pocket!)

"Nah, she's sweet. Ripe as a plum. Ready for it. *Wants* it."

He hauled at my jeans. The denim grated my legs like an emery board. Loam-filled air swirled about me. The flash of a snake tattoo.

I thrashed. I flailed. I choked. The dirt was creating a blindfold and soon I couldn't see at all. Tears of shame forced their way between my lashes. I bit my lip. The blood seeped through.

They argued. "What if she's got AIDS?"

They sounded worried. Had I been saved by a split lip?

"Nah, Hank, mate. She's too young."

"I have. I've got AIDS." I spat the words in a desperate spray of sludge, my mind spinning. He'd said *Hank*. Was the anxious one Hank With Attitude? Angela's Hank? "You'll die if you touch me!"

My head snapped back as he hit me. I began to make dirt-filled, hacking noises. My chest heaved, contracted on the inward breath. Carrot juice spittle, salty with blood, slid onto my cheek—one long red-orange teardrop.

"I go first? Or you?" They were arguing again.

Hope soared. These bogans sounded like amateurs. Was this their first time? Was it a dare? Were they tossing a coin right now?

My brain moved into slow motion. Why were they taking so much time? I almost wished they'd get on with it, make up their minds one way or the other. I gave my body one last hopeful thrust. Kicked out with the strength I had left.

Sweaty hands slipped away. My foot connected. A high screeching sound. A yelping, like a dog hit with a stick.

"Jeez. She got me."

"Mate. C'mon. Let's get out of here. I'm packin' death."

"Bitch! Look, I can't walk."

"Yeah. Course ya can. Carrrmon, mate."

"Didn't happen to you, but."

"Let's go. What if someone comes?"

"Naaah. No one'll come."

"*Told* ya. I'm packin'."

"Too good to waste, mate. She's a virgin slut."

How did they know? Was there a sign on my forehead? VIRGIN!

I listened to them bicker. At least I'd diverted them. Perhaps they'd forget about me. Small child theory surfaced in my mind: *lie doggo, close your eyes*. Ipso facto—you *cannot* be seen.

They kept arguing. I kept praying.

A spray of sandy loam squirted between my legs, spewed onto my stomach. Running footsteps. The ground vibrated.

A voice, a male voice. Older. Someone else was there.

"*Stop*. Come 'ere. What is you doing?"

The words were spoken in a strong accent. A French accent?

I kept my eyes tight shut, hoping the bogans had gone. The sounds of footsteps faded, disappeared into the distance. There was thrashing through ti-trees. Silence.

"You is okay?" A man was bending over me. He looked concerned.

Relief mixed with embarrassment as I floundered my way up. Sand spurted when I yanked at my clothing. My eyes stung, watered like a tap. My mouth throbbed but I felt hope. This voice seemed different, safer. I hoisted my jeans. He reached to help. I hopped on one leg, and dragged them up as quickly as I could.

I rubbed my eyes, smeared dirt on my face.

"I thought you might've been Jack Bradfield," I blubbered.

"You want whisky?" He sounded flummoxed.

"Whisky?"

A wincey smile in his voice. "Jack Daniel."

"Noooo. It's someone I'm afraid of."

"I not Jack Daniel. But I 'ave some in my place."

I was confused. Why was he banging on about Jack Daniel?

"You not want whisky?" He sounded kind. "I sink you need whisky."

I wiped my hand across my nose. I was so ashamed the pores of my skin hurt.

He seemed ill at ease. "You is much injured?"

His arm wrapped around my shoulders and, through a blur, I saw it was the man from the beach, the one with the expensive gear. I'd been gazing at his boat shoes.

"I'm okay." I seemed to be in one piece, but—"I've lost my bomb."

"Bomb? I can get it for you?" He cleared his throat. "You wish to see doctor?"

"Please leave it." I just wanted outta there.

"Show me direction of your dwelling." He tweaked his shades as he talked. "Per'aps not so good to walk in bushes. You must be careful, borrow a road."

Borrow a road? I didn't know whether to laugh, or cry, or barf on his boat shoes. Instead, I argued. "But," I began, before deciding it'd be crass to get on the wrong side of my saviour with the fractured English. His arm made me feel secure. He smelled different from the boys I knew. Not a Stefan Becker locker room smell, but a man smell. A whiff of after-shave, a hint of foreign cigarettes. An odour I seemed to remember from my childhood.

He said his name was Marcel Manet. "Ze police?"

Uh-uh. "No way," I said. To distract him from thoughts of the fuzz, I added, "I saw you climbing the steps to the house on Ti Point. Have you bought it?"

He shook his head. "I am renting for a small while."

Once more he offered to see me home, but I didn't want Namilly to find out about the slam job in the ti-tree bushes. I waved good-bye.

Shaken and shivery, I jogged off down the road wondering how I'd ever be able to study that night.

As I ran I asked myself: *had this guy followed me*? And if so, why?

Chapter 6

Night-time, every muscle ached. The inside of my lip was raw and swollen. I'd scrubbed the dirt from every pore, scoured until the soap became thin and sloppy. My skin had a rosy glow, yet I still felt dirty. Those bogans had seen my knickers, slavered at the sight. And they'd called me a virgin slut. *How could you be a slut if you were still a virgin*? I wondered.

I huddled in the bathroom until Namilly banged on the door. She didn't quiz me. She seemed as preoccupied as ever.

Had my encounter with the bogans turned me into an instant skank? Was I now the town slut? Had they been given the word I was easy? Worse, would they spread the rumour? Diss me?

I couldn't stop thinking about the man who called himself Marcel Manet. From the pungent smell of his cigarettes, I knew there'd been a man of some sort in my life. But my brain was like an unused exercise book whenever I tried to think back before Namilly. I didn't even recall the journey—there'd always been boats and sea voyages. Now, we were still by the sea but without the boats. Still in a place with pine trees, but the pine trees were fatter, not skinny ones with feathered branches huddling in bunches from the trade winds.

My mind was stuffed with too many questions. Unable to sleep, I clambered out of bed. I went to my computer, booted up. Jules was not in the chat room.

I accessed my mailbox. Only one email, asking me to join a flash mob incident in Kingston. I pressed the Delete button, shot it to the rubbish bin.

Feeling hungry, I wandered into the kitchen, grabbed a handful of macrobiotic rice and began to munch. While gouging bits from between my teeth with my fingernail, I spied cockroaches—offspring of Namilly's sunroom kitchen cockroach?—huddled on the bench. And my bomb was back in the bushes.

I wielded a wooden spoon. Splat! Hank gone. Splat! His friend dead. I broke a sprig off the chocolate mint plant and mooched back to my bedroom, chewing.

Gazing out the window past the sea of rippling canna leaves, I saw a shadow shifting near the grevillea cubby I'd played in as a kid, the place where I'd spent hours pretending I had a father, mother, brothers and sisters. The person shape came closer. I nearly choked on a chocolate mint leaf. *Not Hank? Not his friend?* Goose bumps rippled up my arms.

A horse's whinny rattled through the night air. A tail swished, and I relaxed. Hair gleamed in the moonlight and I saw it was Win, headed for the canna patch. She lowered herself, and sat down.

From where I stood, Win seemed gungy. Had she been studying, and decided to take a break before she turned in? Life for Win must be bleak, I told myself, on her own with no one to talk to but Bill Einstein—decrepit as a gee-gee, but whizzo for a chat.

She dragged something from her pocket, and raised it to her lips. Grog? No, the bottle was too shiny, too delicate. Medication, perhaps? We were at the stress end of the year and Win was hoping to enrol in vet science at uni.

Should I go into the garden, say hi? I wondered. She was probably lonely. Then again—she could be distant sometimes.

I decided to brave it. I estimated Namilly would be dead to the world. I'd watched her sip her Sticky Berry dessert wine that evening and seen another cockroach, dead as the ones I'd squashed, wallowing unnoticed in the bottom of her glass. "Roaches, there're none of those things in *my* kitchen." I'd choked back a snort.

Closing the wire door carefully behind me, I padded through the grass. Engrossed in her thoughts, Win looked strung-out for someone whose future beckoned so enticingly.

"What's new pussycat?" I sat down beside her.

She started. "Geez, Gen. You gave me a fright. What're you doing here?"

"I live here, remember?"

"Can't you sleep, either?" Her voice was warm.

"A bad thing happened to me this afternoon and it's playing on my mind." I sniffed. "Phew, it stinks here. Those cannas are right over the septic tank."

"Yeah. The smell, like, reminds me of Bill Einstein." Win sounded mellow.

"You sick?" I asked.

"Just zonked," she said.

Looking around, I was unable to see the bottle she'd been carrying. Had she thrown it into the canna patch? Win's eyes were shiny. Her breath was sweet. She smelled like Namilly's Sticky Berry dessert wine, only more floral.

"Your mum back yet?"

"Yeah, for about half an hour. Then she went away again."

"The late plane? Like, so hardly worth the effort."

"Nah, Gen, frustrates me. Hardly worth the effort at all. She's wandering the world, talks to all *sorts* of people."

"Lifestyle things?"

"Bit like that." Win's T-shirt was crusty, with food clinging to one of her sleeves. She was far from her immaculate self that evening.

"Bill Einstein been mucking with your gear again?"

"Bingo!"

"He seems to do that a lot."

"Yeah." Win's face went soft; we were on her favourite topic now. "I let him into the backyard." She rolled her eyes. "*Big* mistake. He got bored, yanked everything off the line. I had to do all the washing again. Don't blame him, but. He never means it, just a touch of the—"

"Touch of the what?"

"Nothing. Oldness, I s'pose."

Win always spoke as if Bill Einstein were a human being. Her conversation could be like a maze. If you knew where the end was, you understood where she was coming from.

"What's with the food?" I pointed to her sleeve. It looked as if a kid had flipped a spoonful of bubble and squeak at her.

"Bill Einstein knocked my arm while I was feeding him."

"Baby food? Pumpkin for a horse?"

"He *must* be spoon fed, Genna." Win's mouth was a thin line. "And he so *needs* his pumpkin."

I was nearly blown away by her boronia breath.

"Okay, don't get your knickers in a knot."

She calmed down. "It's difficult for her—I mean *him*—to graze these days."

I had never heard of a horse being spoon fed before. "You cook dinner for your mother tonight as well, after she arrived from the airport?"

I'd hit a nerve.

"What's this? The third degree?" Win seemed to quiver. "MYOB. Why are you so concerned about my eating habits?"

"Sorreee." I was afraid of offending her further but I was unable to help myself. A lot bothered me about her life.

"Phone still off the air?"

"Yeah," she glared. "*Still* off the air."

"As you don't have one, and I don't understand why." She frowned but I ploughed on, "How does your mother, like, order a taxi?"

"Mobile phone, airhead." She pushed herself up. "And if you understood anything at all about the life of a fashion editor, you'd *know* they receive obscene phone calls the whole time. It goes with the territory. You cannot afford to have a landline."

Win began to walk away. She stopped and looked at me, as if about to say something.

"Win, would you say I was, like, a *skank*?"

"Skankiness is a matter of perception. If you feel like one, you are one. You can be skidy sometimes. But skank?" Her gaze took in my crumpled trackie daks, raggy sweatshirt. She was suddenly interested. "What bad thing happened today?"

"Ah, I nearly got raped in the ti-tree scrub. And the name of one of them—" I decided not to tell her his name was Hank.

I felt like throwing up. That smell in the canna patch was worse than the empty cans on the other side of the fence.

"Look, I've got multi stuff on my plate. I can't take your problems on board, too." She chewed her fingernail. "Something else you're not telling me?"

"Well," I said, disappointed she wasn't more interested, "there's Fat Betty Stubbs. She's sniffing around Stefan again."

Win's eyes did a belly dance.

"A Jenny Craig course and she's a potential dudette," I added.

"Stuff happens, Gen."

Why did I get the impression Win was talking about herself? She gave me a funny look again, as if there was something she wanted to tell me. Nothing to do with the bogans, nothing to do with Elizabeth.

"ZZZZZZZZZZZ," she said. "I'm off."

Chapter 7

Tears ran down my cheeks, but my eyes refused to open. A heavy weight. I was unable to push the weight away. A lid slammed shut. The light was pale, the air thick. An iron band constricted my chest. A white goose sat beside me, hard against my head. My head hurt. I thumped, but the lid refused to open. Win loomed with her little bottle. I yelled, screamed, banged with my fists. *Help me, Win. There's a snake tattoo. And a goose …*

The box plants, sitting on the sofa lid, banged back. They made a clunky sound.

☆ ☆ ☆

I lurched up from the dream in a lather of perspiration. My bedclothes were drenched, my quilt damp. I could hear the dull clink of a shovel coming from the garden, a spade shafting into root-bound earth.

I glanced at my bedside clock.

3.30am! Who was digging at this hour?

I clambered from my bed, and peered out the window. Yes, someone was definitely working in the garden. And there was only one person who did that at our place: Namilly.

The moon had slipped behind a cloud and it was difficult to see. I strained. No, too dark.

Without warning the moon shone, fleetingly, like a light flicked on. I dimly made out my mother, turning clods of earth in the canna patch. She was burying trash, or junk of some sort. Her movements were jerky, as if it were urgent. What was so urgent that it couldn't wait until daylight?

I crept back to bed, and wriggled myself into a comfortable position. I hauled on my quilt, hugged it to my chin, thinking about the sofa dream. I'd been having heaps of sofa dreams lately, and they scared me. Was my inner self trying to tell me something?

With a start, I recalled having neglected to clip the box plants on my windowsill. Should I creep out, and grab the secateurs now?

I thought about it for a microsecond. Nope, Namilly'd see me and know I'd seen her. I pulled the quilt over me and shivered until the spade noise ceased, until dawn began to break.

And dust motes hung suspended like honey droplets.

Chapter 8

The computer screen shimmied. The water-feature was in full swing as I sweated over my studies. The Symbol Insert wasn't working properly and my accents were all over the place. With the Roman five making a V to represent *Venir*, was V TRAMPS AND ME the right mnemonic to help with my verbs? Or was it V TRAMPS DREAM'N? Both worked, I guess. Uh-oh, they didn't. *Retourner* was missing in the first mnemonic. *Revenir*? *Devenir*? *Rentrer*? They were extensions of *Venir* and *Entrer*.

My head reeled and popped with frustration, interspersed with flashes of the previous night: Namilly Perrier digging in the canna patch.

I decided to take a break from memorising French verbs which took 'to be' in the perfect tense. I logged on to *babesinwoods.com*. Still no Jules.

Leaving the screen flickering I pulled on a pair of cut-offs, and slid my feet into an old pair of thongs. I was unable to stop thinking about my close shave in the ti-tree bushes, about the need to keep the details from Namilly.

I should go to the beach, try to find the man who'd rescued me, thank him, and warn him about not saying anything to my mother. I had to be certain he'd keep his mouth shut if he ever met her. I was also curious to know more about him. Where was he from? Why was he in Ravella?

☆ ☆ ☆

The sand was damp from the rain. The beach was deserted that afternoon as I headed for the bathing boxes and crouched beneath the eaves. A fine mist hung in the air, a sort of fuzzy rain pushed along by the southerly. I shivered, wishing I'd worn a sweater.

I could hear someone speaking on a mobile phone. "*Salut*, Jacques." There was low talking in French, and then he switched to English. "*Non*, not beautiful like Sandrine. She 'as bad hairs." Switch to French. "*Salut, bye*." Silence. A sigh.

Well, somebody had a bad haircut. Somebody wasn't beautiful like Sandrine.

The rich odour of foreign cigarettes drifted from the vicinity of the Becker's bathing box. I decided to leave. It wouldn't do for Marcel Manet to think I'd been eavesdropping. I set off across the sand, gripping my thongs, determined to hotfoot it before he sighted me.

"*Salut, mademoiselle.*"

I froze.

"Geneviève is your name?"

Marcel wore a pair of immaculate white shorts, a shirt with Blanc Bleu embroidered on its pocket. His navy-blue boat shoes were neatly tied. His shades were perched in the middle of his forehead in the European way. His teeth were set in a perfect smile as he moved towards me, briefly stopping to grind his butt into the sand. I noticed his legs were hairy.

"Who, me? Sorry, my name is Genna."

"Ah, you not tell me you is Geneviève?"

"Nup. It's always been *Genna*."

"I see. I not well understand. Come, sit." He patted a nearby step. "You first lovely lady I meet in Ravella." He seemed anxious to be friendly.

The incident in the ti-tree bushes flooded into my mind. I began to go hot all over, embarrassed to have met him in such a compromising situation. A feeling of unease crept through me. Had I been wrong to find his presence comforting? Was he another Jack Bradfield, a voyeur, but with a foreign accent? Reluctantly I edged to the steps of the bathing box and sat down beside him.

"You not Geneviève, never?" Monsieur Manet was persistent.

"*Never*. It's always been Genna. In fact, I have a problem with the name. Geneviève kinda gives me the creeps."

"*Ah*. Why is so?"

"Dunno. Just does."

"Okay, lovely lady called Genna. I hear you swear in French."

I shrugged.

"You understand French, a little?"

"A bit," I said. "My final exam's in a few days."

"Your parents are French?"

"No, but Namilly sometimes makes me talk French when we eat."

"Namilly?"

"My mother." It seemed inappropriate to tell a stranger I was adopted.

"Why you speak French when you eat?" He looked puzzled.

"Good a time as any." I shrugged again. (I was getting plenty of practice at shrugging.)

"Your muzzer," he asked, leaning towards me, "you tell her what 'appen yesterday?"

"Nope." I felt the flush rise again.

Marcel lifted his hands in exasperation. "You *must* talk about it. Ozzerwise you suffer ver-ry much."

"S'pose, but we're talking about it now."

I tried to force myself to relax. He was right. I should discuss it with someone, but not with Namilly. And probably not with him. It seemed a good idea to change the subject. I decided to confide in him about my mother digging in the canna patch.

"Why would someone, in your opinion, dig in the garden in the middle of the night?"

He smiled. "Maybe zey cannot sleep, maybe 'ave somesing to put beneath ground. Your cat is died?"

"No, there's no cat."

His blue eyes were busy as he began to warm to the subject. "Cat is bitten by snake, per'aps?"

I shook my head.

"She is eat poison?"

I shook my head again.

"She very old?"

Why was he fluffing on about our non-existent cat? Was he embarrassed at having seen me half-undressed?

"There's definitely no cat." I was starting to stress out.

"Pity," he said. "Who is it dig in night-time?"

"My mother."

"Eh, you ask 'er," he beamed. "You ask fazzer, too. Maybe it was 'im."

"There is no father."

"No fazzer?" Marcel looked curious.

"Dunno about him. I've been told my mother passed away though."

"But you say she dig in garden in dark?"

"Namilly isn't my real mother. I'm adopted."

There, it was out. Boy, had I stuffed up by staying and talking to him. He was asking way too many questions.

"'ow she die?"

"Namilly doesn't talk about it much." I hesitated. "She was young, I think."

"I is sorry." He sounded genuinely disappointed, but why should he care if my birth mother was dead? I asked myself.

"Your fazzer?"

"Sorry, can't help you." I began to wonder if he was from Human Services.

"Your Namilly, she never tell you about 'im?"

I shook my head.

"Would you be unhappy if you find 'e die during big fighting?"

Was he doing some sort of market research?

"Are you from Human Services?" I asked.

He didn't answer, but his next question gave me a jolt. "Namilly, she is your *nounou*?" His voice was abrupt, as if it was important to him.

"'Course not." I stared at him. "You only have a nanny if your parents go off and do stuff, like party. My mother was poor, she worked for Namilly. She never could've afforded a *nounou*."

"Where she used to work, your natural muzzer? In France?"

"No, in the South Pacific."

"DOM TOM?"

"If you mean French territory, yes. Noumea."

"I is from DOM TOM, too." He looked thoughtful.

"A Caldoche, born in New Caledonia and identify with the place?"

He nodded.

"How weird. I'm a Caldoche, too."

Some coincidence. *I'm* lying on the ground in a total mess and *he* happens to come along—two Caldoche in the same place at the same time. An idea blasted through my head like a meteor. What if this man was my dad? It'd explain why he was in Ravella.

"D'you have any kids?" My insides twisted as I asked the question.

He tried to make a joke of it. But I was serious. Had he come to claim me from Namilly? By now, I was ninety-nine percent certain that Marcel Manet was my natural father. Had he been madly in love with my mother? Had they been young, torn apart by a terrible fate?

My head began to swim. I would change my name to Genna Manet. I would return to the island where I'd been born, live with Marcel and start a new life. I needed to know everything about him.

"What d'you do when you're not hanging out, um, on the beach?"

He blinked. "I is consultant."

"Like Skye Becker? Stefan's sister is a laundry consultant at the Last Gasp Guesthouse."

"I working with Monsieur Jacques Forestier." He made a money sign with his fingers.

"How wonderful!" I was proud my father worked with the movers and shakers.

He pulled a packet of cigarettes from the pocket of his shirt. Blue, it was inscribed with the words Gauloises Blondes. On it was a sketch of a winged helmet, like the Astérix character on one of Mrs B's music boxes. He placed one in his mouth, and lit up using a flash gold lighter.

I frowned.

"What is matter?" He stared at me.

"Smoking, it's bad for your health. Unless it's chop-chop, of course." I dreaded losing my newfound father to lung cancer.

"My fazzer die of cancer right—" He prodded his finger into his throat, and blew a cloud of smoke into the air. "Bloody awful."

"I think you should stop then."

"I try but after I meet you," he said, wiggling his fingers, "pouf! I smoke whole pack."

So, he *had* been bothered by the rough up in the ti-tree bushes. "You won't tell her about it?"

He raised an eyebrow.

"Namilly. *Please* don't say anything about what happened. She'll chuck a spazz. And it's still freaking me out."

For the first time, he seemed stuck for words. I leaned over, gave him two kisses in the French way. "*Au revoir, Papa.*"

"I look so old for you to call me *Papa*?" he murmured, shaking his head as he reached into his pocket.

He pulled out a wad of crumpled notes, extracted two fifties. "For make them better." He pointed to my hair, and handed me the money.

My feet hardly touched the ground. I flew up the path to the top of the cliff. My father was here. And he was the sexiest man in the whole world. Hot.

Chapter 9

I tucked the fifty-dollar notes safely in my underwear drawer, rolling them up in a leopard-print G-string I'd bought for a special occasion. They'd be safe there, I reasoned. I planned to go to Kingston and have a new haircut, buy spangled clips with the money left over.

Peering at my image in the mirror, through the fly specks and salty spots, I pulled my hair this way and that.

Marcel was right. My 'do was stringy and uneven. Just three weeks ago I'd cut it myself with the kitchen scissors, held it in clumps and chopped.

My hair was scraggy, a sort of girl-mullet thing. I liked the gamine style around the edges. But *he* minded, and as he could well be my father, I planned to do something about it.

I examined my features. Was mine the kind of face only a mother could love? Did he see me that way? My birth mother must have been small-boned and olive-skinned like me. Same ravishing smile, same soulful eyes.

I decided to tell Namilly the news. She had disappeared earlier that morning and not returned. I should seek her out, and give her the latest info: *my dad had turned up.*

I jogged past the pine where Namilly had buried my first Serge Gainsbourg disc, deeming it depraved. Hetty Geiger, adolescent bootlegger, had a mega supply of pirated copies. So I forked out fifty cents for another. Then another. In the end, tired of burying the discs, Namilly gave up. She stuffed cotton wool in her ears and retreated to her plants, tamping angrily with her tin trowel.

She was not in the canna patch. I glanced inside the grevillea cubby. Not there, either.

I heard the cranking of the back gate, the clank as it closed shut, and Namilly appeared. Her shoulders drooped. Her hair stood on end. I could smell pee, overlaid with the wholesome odour of NapiSan. Her eyes were blank. She looked as if Dr Death had placed his hand upon her shoulder.

The joy I'd felt at discovering my father was swept from my mind. Had Namilly been at the Zabaglione Woollen Shop, discussing the dynamics of her problem with her friend Mrs B?

"How are you feeling, Ma?" I touched her gently on the arm.

She shrugged my hand away.

"Sure there's nothing wrong?"

She was silent. Time to tell her my news.

"Namilly, I've found him."

"Found who? That Stefan hasn't been hanging around, chaining himself to the front fence like a dog again?"

I stared. Who was *I* meant to be then? Stefan's fave tree? Or a light pole, perhaps? Why did she hate him so much? Was she afraid we'd jump into the sack? I put Stefan firmly to the back of my mind.

"Nope, someone else."

"Well?"

"Papa's here, in Ravella." I felt the triumph in my voice.

"What papa?" She frowned.

"The papa from Noumea, my father."

Namilly's look was apprehensive. Her face flushed right down her neck, the colour spreading along her arms like a stain. The hot flush faded.

"Don't be ridiculous, Genna. You've been spending too much time in chat rooms. Stick to your verbs, to the basics, the things one can quantify. Your imagination will get you into trouble." She pushed her heavy gold signet ring into my ribs. "And don't talk to strange men on the beach when you're by yourself."

I gasped with disappointment.

The uncertainty was now washed from her eyes. "Stacked the wood, have you? Watered the topiaries? They need a clip. I pay you—"

"The woodpile's fine. And I watered the miniatures this morning. I'll clip them now. I know they're overdue."

"You'd better have another look at that wood."

Namilly strode off towards the house, leaving me examining the woodpile. Three logs had rolled to the ground since I last checked and it wasn't even windy.

Namilly's frame was sphinxlike. She slammed the door shut behind her.

I re-stacked the wood, chopped some extra kindling with a tomahawk, and placed the splintered pieces within easy reach. Summers were often chilly in Ravella.

With spider webs gusting in my face, I grabbed the secateurs from the shed, and stretched up to the terracotta pots housing the plants upon my windowsill. I began to shape them carefully, trying not to bruise the leaves. I stood back. Assessed. Snipped again, cursing as I clipped. *Didn't Namilly know I was in the middle of my final examinations?*

Baby leaves soon gloved my sneakers in frothy green. The haircut I was giving my plants was as neat as my own would be.

Sweaty and deflated, I trudged to my room to do battle with my French verbs. Before burying myself in my studies, I eased open my underwear drawer. I pushed aside my bikini pants and crop tops. I was hanging out to see the money again, to savour it, to sniff the plastic and recall my meeting with Marcel. The notes were not there. My leopard-print G-string was empty.

I opened all my drawers, chucked out clothes willy-nilly. Pilled jumpers piled in a tangled heap on the floor. School ties with food spots lolled around like stripy snakes. I threw everything I possessed to the boards, searched in sleeves, poked in pockets. I even looked under my bed, pushing the dust aside with my fingers.

No fifty-dollar notes. Had Namilly taken them? I needed to confront her.

The frypan was cold in the sunroom kitchen, the waffle iron empty. I found her crouched on our living room floor with the lid of the hollow sofa thrown back. She was pushing her cans around on the polished boards again. She was making grid patterns, circles, lines and isosceles triangles. Rectangles and hexagons. And all the while she kept murmuring to herself.

I grew giddy as I watched her.

The tin of pickled pork was no longer there. Had she eaten it, before hurling the empty container over the fence onto the smelly pile the other side? I trudged back to my room. This was not the time to quiz her about the disappearance of my dosh.

I decided to boot up, go online before I tangled with my V TRAMPS.

Jules was in the chat room. We talked for so long my fingers began to tingle. I told him about Marcel. I told him about Namilly. I told him about all my problems.

"We have so much in common," he said.

Chapter 10

I tossed and turned, unable to sleep, my mind fizzing with Jules and the perfect tense. If only my own past were as perfect as that perfect tense. All my friends knew their birth mothers, but mine was a V TRAMPS DREAM'N sort of mother—text-book theoretical.

Was I one of several, I wondered. Were there siblings? Or was I an only child? If Namilly knew, she wasn't saying. Anyway, it was doubtful I could believe anything she told me, in view of her current dodgy behaviour.

I began to recite my V TRAMPS DREAM'N to help me sleep. *Venir, Tomber, Rester, Aller, Monter, Partir, Sortir* …

The word '*sortir*' flashed like a neon sign. Yesss. I should go out, dig in the canna patch and discover what my mother had been burying.

I pushed my feet into an old pair of thongs, grabbed a jar of Vaseline and made for the back door. Namilly's breathing was heavy and even as I crept past her room.

I smeared Vaseline onto the hinge and eased myself out.

The knob of the shed door was stiff. I jiggled and smeared until it creaked open. I flicked the switch. The globe was dead. I searched around with my fingers for a shovel, flinching as spider webs brushed against my face. Grasping the splintery handle of the spade, I set off. The canna patch churned darkly before me, and I tried to recall the exact spot I'd seen her digging. From memory, it was smack bang in the middle. Not close to the fence, nor near the rotting canned food, but in the centre.

I took a breath and plunged in.

I shafted the blade into the soil. The roots of the plants resisted the metal and pushed back at me. I tried a second spot. A third. I kept going until I felt the ground become softer. The leaves caressed my arms as if willing me to continue. But the earth remained stubbornly root-bound. I moved closer to the lawn's edge, probed in sharp jabs.

By now, my hair was stuck to my head like seaweed. I joggled the strands from my eyes, and swung the shovel hard.

About to give up, I felt a sudden click. Eureka! This was it.

My excitement subsided. The blade of the shovel had become wedged. I'd struck a stone. Either that, or the metal of our septic tank.

I wiggled my instrument. A sour smell wafted up, tickling my nasal hairs. I pushed the back of my hand against my nose to stop the sneeze. Toiled on.

I struck another hard object. But there was no click this time. It was more of a clink, a high sound. I reached down, loosened the earth, and slid my fingers beneath it. Levered. I picked up the object and examined it. I held a bottle, a tiny bottle with a sweet smell. I brushed the earth off the elegantly shaped glass to reveal a perfume bottle, an empty one. I groaned. Was this the big mystery? The bottle could've been there forever.

Then again, the glass looked new. I could see no scratches on its surface. It glinted in the moonlight as I squinted at the label: Polka Dot. I dropped the bottle back, covered it over with loose soil.

Why would Namilly bury a perfume bottle? Why not throw it out with the garbage? Why not hurl it over the fence with her cans?

I jabbed the shovel in the ground in frustration. Another clink. Another perfume bottle? I dug frantically. Polka Dot again. How odd.

I kept digging. Sweat began to pour down my face in long drops. I unearthed a third bottle. Then a fourth. Fifth. Sixth. Soon I was surrounded by perfume bottles, an ocean of them. And not all were Polka Dot. There were tiny French samples. Miss Dior. Addict. First. Some brands I'd never heard of. But most were Polka Dot. And all were empty.

My breathing was becoming raspy. I felt faint from lack of sleep. I needed to get out of here in case Namilly came looking for me. Heaping the bottles into the ground, I smoothed the soil over and patted it down as evenly as I could.

Retourner, I whispered to myself. *Entrer*. Go into the house.

I fled to the back door, my chest encircled by an iron band. I heaved the shovel through a gap in the boards as I passed, planning to put it in the shed later.

I crept to my room, scrambled beneath the quilt. Recited verbs to calm myself down. Would Namilly see I'd disturbed the earth? A shiver went through me.

I heard a sudden tinny sound, spits on the roof. Drops turned to rain. The heavens opened up, until it was pelting down. My body turned slaggy with relief. That churned earth would turn to mud, become packed hard by the wind and sun. In a few short days, she'd never notice.

I tossed and turned, bothered by what I'd discovered. I was living with a crazy person, a loony tune who buried perfume bottles in the middle of the night for no good reason, instead of putting them in the garbage like everybody else.

Could it be the onset of some terrible disease?

Like depression?

Chapter 11

Late next morning the phone burped in my ear. Angela Rasmussen was up for air. She sounded chirpy, apparently not bothered by those looming final examinations.

"Finished with *Merde! The French Your Teachers Never Taught You*?" I asked, knowing I'd need it for my oral.

Angela's voice sashayed through the airwaves. "Better than the Kama Sutra," she said.

As if. What would *she* know?

"I'll give you some hairclips I bought in Kingston," she pleaded.

"Okay. You can have it another coupla days." Would I own Angela's entire wardrobe before too long? And she … left naked with Jason? Angela wasn't even an aspiring slut. She'd graduated top of the class. And where did that leave me? With creepy bogans attacking me in the bushes?

Shivering at the thought, I rushed to the bathroom and peered at my image in the mirror. Between the black spots, I saw that Marcel was right. I needed a new look. I was too old for the Piaf-of-the-gutters-of-Paris thing. I should attempt to fix it. What would my father say if I bumped into him on the beach, which I planned to do sometime, and I'd done nothing to my hair? I could hardly say I'd mislaid his money.

Namilly was brooding in her sunroom kitchen. A pile of uneaten waffles wafted black smoke into the air. Had she seen me in the canna patch last night? Been watching from her window? Decided to say nothing until it suited her purpose? But why bury perfume bottles? It had to be connected with her deteriorating health. There was no other plausible explanation.

I fiddled with my strands. Should I make a French plait? Namilly used to do one for me. If *she* knew how, it couldn't be too hard.

I split my hair into three thick lumps at the back of my head, and began to weave. Soon my circulatory system was threatening to shut down. My fingers began to fritter, flop around my hands like tired sausages. I began to wonder if it was worth the effort.

Finished at last, I flicked an elastic band around the base, examined my reflection. Well, *nobody* would rape me now. I was formidable. Neat. Intimidating. A full-on, old-fashioned nerd. And Marcel would never guess I'd not had a professional coiffure. I could safely bump into him accidentally-on-purpose.

I thought of going online, but decided I'd wasted enough of my time. I went back to my V TRAMPS DREAM'N, examining them for their intransitivity. *Venir*—intransitive. *Tomber*—both intransitive and transitive. (It made sense, like me—I'd fallen off the back of a truck as a baby.) I was in the midst of ticking off the verbs when there was a tap at the bedroom door.

"I'll be in the garden." Namilly hesitated, and then launched into one of her Stefan diatribes. "That Becker boy's chained himself to our front gate. *Do* something."

My mother was making canine comments about my mate again. I needed to rescue Stefan before he suffered third degree burns from sunlight exposure.

On the way out, I grabbed two banana passionfruits from the vine. Offered him one through the cyclone wire.

He shook his head.

I split the skin with my thumbnail, poked my tongue inside the cleft, and sucked out the tart pips.

His pale eyes stared at me, blue against the mountain of zinc cream. Would Stefan ever be comfortable with making the commitment to come through our gate? Or would Namilly terrify him for the rest of his life?

He was clad in a new white Boomdogger T-shirt, and I could see welts on his ears where the zinc cream had worn off. My heart went out to him. Life must be poxy for a Becker from Northern Europe, I told myself. There were advantages in being a Caldoche, after all. Should I tell him about the perfume bottles among the cannas? I decided not to. He'd probably just think it was women's business.

He didn't comment on my new coiffure, didn't blush with pleasure at seeing me. He looked pale and intense. His bright hair was subdued, neatly plastered down. He thrust an envelope into my hand and hurried off.

I eyed the missive. Had Stefan just delivered divorce papers? Were we no longer friends on an official basis? Had he proposed to Fat Betty?

I ran inside, and ripped the letter open. It was not what I'd expected. Gasp, gasp, GASP.

A shaky heart was sketched in red on cheap lined paper, creating the impression of being rent into a squillion slabs. Within the outline, the letter was formal. I devoured my first words of adoration:

Dear Genna, he wrote, *you are the only person I will ever wish to hang out with even if I live to one hundred years within which time I will never wish to hang out with anybody else much at all or go hunt blue ringers as I only like hanging out and doing it with you not even with anybody to whom or to which you might resemble and I hope you feel the same.*

Yours in the hereinafter, Stefan.

There, he'd said it, made his decision. Picked me. Elizabeth Stubbs was out of the picture. I had two guys now—cyberspace Jules, and Stefan Becker. I felt wicked, even more so than when I'd thrashed Elizabeth in the semi-final of the Ravella High tennis championships.

I briefly wondered if Stefan was pulling my leg. I had no idea his writing skills were so average. Aspiring aquaculturalist? Aspiring law-yer, more like. He obviously didn't believe in punctuation muddying his meaning. My first declaration of love was blunt and to the point. I had doubts, though. We'd never really kissed. Well, not kissed in *that* way.

Thinking hard, I put the paper down. Why could we not continue to be mates? I wasn't ready for a serious Jason-type relationship. Screwing up the envelope, I felt a fat bulge. Had he included money to seal the deal?

I shook. A bundle of seashells clattered to the floor. Not any old seashells. These were fat, glossy, luscious cowries. All joined together by sewing cotton. I held the creation up. Too short for my neck, was it a bracelet? I hung the jewellery around my wrist. Nope, too big for a bracelet. Was this shell confection a sort of engagement ring?

I examined his offering closely. Holes had been drilled into these wonderful products of nature. I was touched by Stefan's gesture. I was. Really. Even though it was a tad dorkish.

Where had these shells come from?

I went cold as I knew the answer: Jane Becker.

Stefan's mother owned a shell collection, acquired from Hawaii, Tahiti, all over the world. Had he nicked them? Shoved holes through them? (She'd eat me alive if she saw them decorating my body. Tear me into a thousand pieces. Drop me into The Cauldron, where I'd be sucked in chunks past the seismic activity and Palaeozoic rocks of Selwyn's Fault.) What was I meant to do with this—this *thing*, which could only be described as an anklet? Why had Stefan not bought me a silver chain? Or a friendship ring? Something more traditional.

Face it, Stefan was stingy. He'd only been forced to purchase sewing cotton. And that had probably been whacked from his mother's mending basket.

I had only one alternative, to end this relationship before I was in too deep. Full-on commitment wasn't for me. Anyway, the rough up in the ti-tree bushes had made me iffy about physical closeness.

I decided to tell Namilly. I would tell her I was breaking the whole thing off between me and my mate. She'd be rapt. It would make her day—bluey'd no longer be hanging around the gate with his blue ringers. No more dog comments. Our lives would be more peaceful.

I paused. Or would our lives be more boring?

I pondered. Stefan'd taken up seashell threading for me. I'd never thought of him as a big girl's blouse before.

Was my mate less blokey than I'd imagined?

Chapter 12

I placed his anklet in my bottom drawer. I was about to sally forth when I saw footprints in the dust. Big ones, highlighted by the afternoon sun, slanted across the floorboards. Namilly'd been in my room while I was at the front gate talking to Stefan. What had she been looking for?

I poked my finger into one of the pots. The soil was damp. Uh-oh, another unspoken recrimination.

The back door slapped shut behind me as I sauntered towards the canna patch, trying to look calm and in control. Trying to look as if I'd never even *thought* of digging in there.

I peered among the leaves. No sign of Namilly, but the earth was beginning to recover. Lumpy and ragged, fine roots were pushing through. A few more sunny days and you'd never know I'd been poking around with my shovel.

The overnight rain had swelled the stench from the septic tank. I stifled a gag. But a ripe pong was good. It might keep her away from that section of the garden.

I pushed aside the branches of the grevillea cubby. Namilly wasn't sweeping leaves in there, either.

Then I saw her, half-hidden by a murraya bush. She was tending impatiens, pulling out the leggy bits. Leaning across to cull the last of the pansies.

Her large frame was bent double and I could hear her muttering to herself: "Sluts." The snap of a stem. "Sparkling combs." Had she overheard my conversation with Angela? "Thrown away like an old sock—she looks at me strangely." A cough. "Roadblocks, soldiers." Heavy breathing. "I told her it was too hard."

I soon realised her words had nothing to do with me.

"Safe, she must be safe, and warm. Food's the answer, diet." A long wheeze, the chink of a trowel. "Cleanliness. I told the girl that. Plants help. Right sort of plants." Her voice trembled.

Namilly stood upright, sniffed, rubbed the back of a gloved hand across her eyes. Her thoughts seemed unconnected to the empty perfume bottles I'd found hidden in the canna patch. And I still didn't understand why they should be there. Was it a scam of some sort involving perfume bottles? Maybe connected to Mrs B? (She sold a space age range of things at the Zabaglione Woollen Shop.) Had Jack helped her bury the empties? No, I'd definitely only seen Namilly digging around in there. And Jack'd never been anywhere near our garden. (He'd not even climbed through my bedroom window to watch me sleep. I would've known; I'd been awake most nights.)

"*Prendre un enfant par la main.*" Namilly's voice was a bass baritone.

A weed landed like a hand grenade on the path beside me, spattering earth across my Reeboks.

Should I ring Human Services, tell them a family member had tipped over the edge? No, I told myself, my complaint would be handballed on to the Tenancy Tribunal.

Another voice came from the direction of the back fence, "'Allo, anybody zere?" It sounded like the Frenchman, Marcel Manet.

"Can I help you?" Namilly extricated herself from her plants, and ambled to greet him. They began to talk.

Panting with nervousness, I hid behind the grevillea cubby. How should I tackle this? Namilly must never know Marcel and I had met. Next thing, she'd find out about the ti-tree sitch.

My hands were clammy. My heart was doing a death rattle. (The dilemma with Stefan was now puddling around at the dregs end of my priority list.) Had Monsieur Manet broken his word, and opted to dob me in? He'd sworn not to say anything. Although, for all *I* knew he might be a pathological liar.

Reality time. Should I stay where I was? Or, should I join them? I decided to confront them. If this man really was my father, I should discover why he was here in Ravella. I took a deep breath, strolled towards them as if I'd been taking a walk, a study break. Taking in the sea air to clear my head.

"There you are, Genna." Namilly's eyebrows tangled in a frown and I got that busted feeling.

Was this to do with my dishabille in the ti-trees?

"There's something you should know," she said.

Uh-oh, now for the lecturing, the vituperation. And a sofa dream would surely follow that evening just when I needed obliterating sleep. Should I take Stefan up on his offer, and run away with him?

"It's something serious." Namilly's brows became one long caterpillar.

I made up my mind to hang on to those cowry shells, use my engagement gift as prayer beads.

Marcel showed no sign we'd ever met.

"What's wrong?" I quavered.

"It's Win."

"What's Win?"

"She's been blown out to sea."

"No way, not into Selwyn's Fault?" I gasped. "Sucked past The Cauldron?"

"Well, out on the Bay."

"Oh, is *that* all?"

Namilly gave a brief scowl.

"I thought it was something worse." Relief flooded through me. Marcel *had* kept his trap shut about the ti-tree incident. "Winnie's done it before. She'll be okay. Move it, you guys."

I charged out the back gate in the direction of the beach. Marcel and Namilly trailed behind. With luck, Win'd be all right.

"Stay cool, stay cool, stay cool," I chanted as I ran.

Chapter 13

I jogged ahead. Marcel followed in a slow lope. Namilly brought up the rear, doing a soft-shoe shuffle in a forward motion.

Namilly puffed and wheezed. The jowls of her face wobbled in time with each step. Attempting to introduce me to Marcel, her lips emitted a long inarticulate sigh.

"We've met," Marcel hacked. Omigod, he'd blown it big time, implied he knew me. Next, she'd be finding out how we met.

"I *told* you not to say anything, *or* to use those things," I hissed over my shoulder. Judging by his cough, Marcel was paying the price for smoking those Gauloises Blondes. I was the healthy one, fit from climbing cliffs and dodging ti-tree bushes. "Use chop-chop if you *must* smoke."

His eyes popped.

"Healthy smoking, nicotine free," I panted. "Bit of bleach, that's all. Mrs B on the highway, you can buy it there. Cheaper even than regular rolling tobacco."

Marcel's face was suffused as he concentrated on negotiating the curve in the road. His boat shoes stayed strangely free of dust.

I kneed open the low wrought-iron front gate and we filed through. Namilly trailed a painful last. Her hair stood upright like desperate fingers waving in sludgy surf.

We scurried over the manicured lawns, scrambled down the stone steps cut into the face of the cliff, and tumbled in a breathless heap onto the rocks.

Marcel pointed to a bobbing dot in the distance.

Apparently Win had taken out the Rasmussen's rubber dinghy, a blind Freddy no-no on the waters of the Bay. And the northerly was pushing her farther out as we stood there.

"Well, when are they coming?" I stared at Marcel. His eyes had a haunted look. "The police, dummy."

"*Merde*," he murmured softly.

"Hellooo. *You didn't ring the water police?*"

"I not know where to ring. Is reason I come to where you live. And I see 'er in garden." He pointed to Namilly. "She is your muzzer?"

I was in no mood for small talk. Soon Marcel would start yammering on about my name, whether it really was Genna. We were wasting time while Win was being swept in the direction of Bass Strait.

Namilly watched the two of us arguing. I would deal with her later. My friend was in dire straits.

"*I'll* do it then. Gimme your house keys. She'll be in Tassie soon."

I snatched the keys from him, and raced up the steps.

Inside, the house smelled of damp. I ran to the phone, dialled 000. "You young idiots are *always* being blown out to sea in this neck of the woods. Be there in twenty," growled the Kingston policeman.

Twenty minutes? Time for a quick squiz.

On the walnut table beside the phone sat a half-full bottle of whisky. Jack Daniel's, the drink Marcel had offered me after my near-rape experience. So he did use the stuff.

The words 'Sour Mash' were printed on the bottle.

A framed photo sat propped against the table lamp: a couple standing before a Mercedes 450SL. The woman, pretty in an airhead way, was clad in a brief bikini. The man wore his dark hair in a military style. This golden couple looked head over heels in love. Who were they?

Apart from the photo, the house had an unlived-in feeling.

I peeked into the kitchen to see two unwashed glasses on the sink. Was there time to investigate the master bedroom? I glanced at my watch. I should be down on the rocks, checking if the Kingston water cops were rescuing Win.

I rushed into the master bedroom to find a neatly made king-sized bed. I peered into the walk-in robe: some shirts, strides, an extra pair jammed into a trouser press.

My spying had revealed little. Monsieur Manet was a tidy guy. He liked whisky. He had spunks for friends. There was little else in that wedding-cake house to fill me in about him.

I was disappointed. Marcel Manet seemed to know a lot about me. Yet I knew nothing about him. And, beneath the designer stubble, in the full light of day with no dirt in my eyes, I could see he was not as old as I'd first imagined.

Was he my father? I was not so sure now.

The guilts began to niggle. Here I was worrying about my origins, while Win was bobbing out on the Bay waiting to be rescued. Worse, if the wind swung to the south, she'd suffer from hypothermia. Turn into a bag of bones. Suffer from starvation. Probably *die*.

Chapter 14

On the rocks Namilly and Marcel were making polite conversation, exchanging names. Marcel appeared intent on ensuring he was up to speed regarding each person's moniker.

"And your name is, *madame*?"

"Perrier." She had a worried look on her face.

He raised an eyebrow, as if to imply my mother had invented her alias in the office of the man who whipped up fake passports in the Latin Quarter of Noumea. Had she seen a bottle of mineral water on his desk? I'd never thought about it before. Perrier was not a common name in this country, last time I checked.

They sized each other up like two bull terriers while I fidgeted and fumed. My friend was scared out there and the water cops seemed to be taking forever.

A boat arced around Ti Point, Mercury twin engines trailing a frothy wake. The Kingston police had arrived. They swung wide towards the rubber dinghy, cut back and edged in.

A neoprene-clad officer, legs astride each rocking vessel, hauled Win into the Sea Ray Sundancer. He wrapped a blanket about her shoulders, lashed the dinghy to the stern of the boat and they headed for shore. Screws reversed. Sand scraped the hull.

"She's safe," I shrieked.

I leaped across the rocks to where a well-muscled young officer was helping Win to disembark. He hauled the old khaki rubber ducky out of the water, and dragged it up onto the beach. This guy was grade-A eye candy.

Ogling his body I took in his slinky skin, which brought Stefan and his imperfections to mind. I'd forgotten about his proposal for hanging out together forever. And now was not the time to tell Namilly, not the time to confide in Win.

Win shook and shivered and sniffed. Her ice-blonde hair was knotty. Her skin was blue. Her mouth was a tense line.

The police issue blanket slipped for a moment, revealing her T-shirt. It was grungy. Yellow food was smeared all over the front like sticky finger painting, worse than on the night beside the canna patch when she said she'd been spoon feeding pumpkin to Bill Einstein. Which puzzled me. Last time I looked, the horse was grazing of his own accord.

Win's cut-offs were ragged, her legs scratched and bleeding. She was a mess, which was unlike her.

I ran to her, threw my arms around her. Her body trembled. She was shaking like the water over Selwyn's Fault, as though she was about to erupt and fizz all over the ground, submerge me in boiling brine and carry me off.

"You're safe," I screamed.

"Yeah," she hiccuped. "Nearly bought it this time, nearly escaped, nearly got outta here."

"*Escaped*?" She hadn't meant to—"You didn't mean to *kill* yourself?"

"Just joking, Gen." She gave me a washed-out smile.

Of course she was joking. Strong people like Win didn't commit suicide. She'd just decided to get away from it all, be on her own for a while. All this study was enough to drive anyone bananas.

"You the lady's mother, ma'am?" The wet-suited policeman jerked his head at Namilly.

His partner with the reflector shades and the married-looking face waited in the Sundancer, diesels idling.

"I'm not her mother," she said, sounding subdued, "but I'll see she gets home safely."

"Time she stopped this caper. It's a waste of our resources." He turned to leave, and then stopped. "Oh, and she had this with her."

He handed Namilly an elegant bottle of perfume and climbed aboard.

The boat took off in a mighty fart of foam, and vanished behind Ti Point. My mind jolted. The guy had handed Namilly a bottle of perfume. Odd. I wondered if it was Polka Dot.

"Where'd you get the perfume?" I asked.

"Ever heard of Duty Free, Gen?" Win's gaze was glassy.

"D'oh, how dumb of me!" I'd never thought of Duty Free. (Alice Winstone must bring home heaps of grouse perfume.)

Marcel's sunnies were gladwrapped to the middle of his forehead, his expression thoughtful. He ambled off, picking his way among the shore boulders. He turned, waved, and climbed the steps in the rock face before disappearing through the weathered gate.

We trudged back along the beach, past the Rasmussen blue bathing box where Angela had been practising her verbs with Jason. Pushed against the shingles until we reached the path.

Namilly heaved and puffed and the thought struck me: this was the first time I could remember her coming to the beach since my 'big toe incident'. She'd never have come for me, but she came for Win. Then again, Win had been in trouble. I still felt jealous.

Outside the two-storey clapboard Win pulled the front door key from her cut-offs, and Namilly did a strange thing. She wrapped her arm around Win and whispered in her ear, surprising me. I'd never thought they were close, and Namilly wasn't a touchy-feely sort of person.

The paint-blistered door closed. I heard the deadlock turn.

A swish noise. Beside the house Bill Einstein, ribs in ridges beneath his furry coat, was grazing for all he was worth. Flicking flies with his tail, nosing at the grass. Nibbling. Moving on. Shaking his mane in a contented fashion.

I stared. Bill Einstein looked fine to me. Why had Win spun me the yarn about spoon feeding him?

Namilly meandered ahead, arms swinging, and I noticed her hands were empty. Where was the perfume bottle given to her by the cop? Had she palmed it back to Win without my seeing? Why be secretive? Was there something going on between them?

Should I return to the beach, I wondered, and discuss these things with Marcel? He hadn't said anything during, or after, the rescue. Simply walked away. Or should I return to my verbs?

Chapter 15

I plumped for my verbs. I knew where I stood with them, whereas I had no idea where I stood with Marcel.

My head buzzed and whirled with questions about Win. Had she tried to kill herself? If so, why? Alice Winstone was away most of the time, but it was a bit far out in the attention-getting department to try to do yourself in. I logged on to distract myself: *whereareyou.com, birthmother.com, babesinwoods.com*. Jules was not in the chat room. I tried *babes. com*—a new website I'd heard about. (It looked porno. The pink haze was suspicious.) I'd begun to leave my name and details in chat rooms, in case anyone had info on my birth mother. I was hanging out for *anything* about her.

I checked my emails. Nothing since the last time I'd looked. I was drawing blanks. (Namilly'd said my birth mother lived not far from the nickel smelter in the southern province of Grande Terre. Not easy researching residents who lived beside a nickel smelter.) Questions began to surface about Win's relationship with Namilly. The mystery of the perfume bottles. The new closeness between them. I decided to suss out Marcel's view of the situation. After all, he was the one who'd alerted us that Win had been blown out on the Bay.

I nearly collided with Namilly emerging from her sunroom kitchen. She skidded an empty baked bean can across the brush fence, missing me by a whisker and trailing slops. The air shimmered with flies. Boy, was *she* harbouring a heap of anger.

A bean landed with a splat at my feet. I was about to diss her, but the vibes gave me pause. Dodging through the garden, I saw her trowel and gloves among the impatiens—unlike *her* to forget her tools, I thought. I jogged past the Winstone clapboard. The blinds were drawn. Bill Einstein grazed in the side paddock.

Opposite, at Grassberger's Guesthouse, residents sat around reading, playing croquet, wrestling with the bias in a game of lawn bowls. Quietly chatting. It looked peaceful being a wrinkly. Skye Becker marched along a path, all short-haired efficiency, fluffy towels tucked under her chin. Unlike her brother, she was smoothly tanned.

Jack Bradfield leaned forward in a stripy deckchair, earnestly talking with a grey-haired man. (His parole officer? Shrink, perhaps?) In his hand, was a massive brown moth. They went into a huddle, examined it, turned it over, peered at the underside. Did he carry this with him when he climbed through bedroom windows? I should ask Hetty the next time I saw her.

Jack Bradfield turned. He smiled at me and pointed to the back of his head, indicating approval of my French plait. He shoved his thumb in the air. Not one person had commented on my new coiffure, but I'd impressed the town Peeping Tom. Did my plait remind him of the caterpillar that gave birth to the monster he was holding?

I removed my sneakers, tied them together, slung them over my shoulder, and skidded down the path to the beach.

No sign of Marcel.

I picked my way around the rocks to The Cauldron where the water hissed and swirled like a washing machine. Surged. Burst forth. Erupted with a crash. Tumbled onto the rocks. Waves collided and curled, crunched their way into the narrow space, and spewed through. Exploded and sucked back in a thunderous gasp. A skimpy residue followed like a bridal train.

The ground rumbled. Was there new seismic activity in Selwyn's Fault? That epicentre was right beneath me. Beyond the frantic fury of froth, the water'd turned calm since Win's close shave. A dolphin arced, late rays of sunshine creating a storm of crystals on its back. I could almost understand why she'd gone there.

A hand touched me on the shoulder, making me start.

"You scared me."

"You is far away. What is matter?" It was Marcel.

"It's Win," I said.

"I cannot hear. Much noise. Come wis me."

He led the way around the corner to a spot where the wind didn't howl. He sat down, and patted the rock beside him.

"She is ve-ry sick," he said.

"Namilly? I know. She's getting past it. Her wheezing's spooky."

"*Non*, your blonde friend. She is very much unwell."

"Win has been strange lately. I thought it was the exams."

"She smoke dope?"

I was stunned at his question. Hetty, perhaps. But Win smoke dope? Never.

"'Er eyes glaze over like sea out zere." He pointed to the distant water.

"I know what you're saying, but she so *totally* wouldn't do that. She only does chop-chop." Thinking of Win being blissed out, my heart began to paddle.

"Maybe you is right," he shrugged. "Anyway, where you buy chop-chop?"

"Mrs B sells it below the counter. It's illegal, really."

"And full of bad sings like mould, straw, and," he said, clenching his teeth, "you say *bleach*?" His eyes went spazball.

"It's cheap. You need something to zap the stress during exams."

Marcel, sick of me fluttering on about fungi-infused fags, Namilly's wheezing and whether Win was wasted, changed the subject. "Your muzzer, she is *poken*?"

"*Poken*?"

"Born in English-speaking country?"

"I s'pose. She doesn't, like, talk about it much."

"I can tell she not *z'oreille*, born in France." Marcel pulled at his ear. "*Z'oreille* is crazy word, from guards who listen. *Calédonie* have convict past, like your country."

"Well, she's a guard sometimes but not French, only speaks it."

I was being drawn into Marcel's web again. The questions, the history lesson. I'd come here to discuss my problems, but I could see he wasn't interested. He didn't even seem hung up anymore by the rock job with the bogans in the ti-tree bushes—still giving me the willies, still keeping me awake at night.

I pushed myself up.

"Stay." He pulled at my hand. "I 'ave story to tell."

Reluctantly, I crouched down again.

"You 'ave heard of *évènements*?"

"The Events, that loony euphemism for war they use in France? Yeah, I've heard of the Events."

"I tell you story," he said.

I hugged my knees to my chest. He began to tell me about Sandrine Bas Salaire de Lyon.

Chapter 16

"Jacques Forestier worry much. Sandrine very crazy daughter." Marcel's voice lilted as he spoke. His vowels were lazy in the island fashion, the 'a' sounds rounded into a soft 'o'. His tone was soothing.

I checked out his boat shoes as I listened.

"Sandrine Forestier like good life. Beautiful daughter of Jacques, money man, she meet Yves-Laurent Bas Salaire de Lyon, soldier, *z'oreille* from metropolitan France. It happen in nakamal—" He saw my blank expression. "—kava bar, in Baie des Citrons. Relaxed by kava, they fall in love. Big wedding follow." He smiled. "Veuve Clicquot, bougna in baskets. The guests dance barefoots on sands of Anse Vata until water of biggest lagoon in world turn red wis morning sun. A warning? For zis couple not live happy ever after.

"Marriage not long finish and ze fight for independence break out. Grande Terre explose. Pouf!" He threw his hands in the air. "Bombs. Everysing.

"Yves-Laurent, very brave soldier, try to make order." He hesitated a moment. "Even fighted in army during birth of 'is baby girl. Then big tragedy come. Near caves on island of Ouvéa, he is wounded, but mosquito finish 'im off. Husband of Sandrine die from dengue fever.

"Crying, crying, for Yves-Laurent, she not wish to keep living."

Marcel gazed across the waters of Port Phillip Bay. The wind ruffled his hair. He looked homesick, as though longing for the tropics where the air was balmier.

"Did she kill herself?" I asked.

"*Non*, but she wish to do it. She lie in darkened room for months. She stay curled up under big white mosquito netting. She eat little. She not see no one. She even not see baby daughter. So *Nounou* do everysing. And nanny very loving." He rubbed his hands together. "She do very good job, put little girl in dresses from Paris with lovely ribbons, pin frangipani in hair. Beautiful.

"After siesta, each day, she lead baby to music kiosk in Place des Cocotiers. Zey listen to music from everywhere. And most popular songs in that times are from Bob Marley and his words of revolution."

He wrinkled his brow as if trying to think back.

"Rasta reign," he continued. "Members of independence movement wear dreadlocks. Wear red bonnets. Smoke corn paper Gauloises. Make roadblocks, make bomb, burn cars. Point rifle at everyone who is in ze way. Independence people are in control." He made a church with his fingers. "For small while.

"Tourist stay away from island. Nickel production slow right down. And reggae play on—"

"Not the music of Serge Gainsbourg?" I interrupted. "*Aux armes et caetera?*"

Marcel struggled up from the depths. He shook his head, sank back into his story.

"*Nounou* and child become no more part of Sandrine's life. Is as if she is died." His face became set. "Baby love to watch cricket, game played by Kanak women in missionary dresses. She follow her best team with *Nounou*. She scream. She clap. She laugh as ladies run up and down ze pitch. Flowers move in pretty ways in trade winds, and zey never miss a single match.

"One day, nanny and child appear no more. Kanak lady cricketers whisper about Caldoche girl." His shoulders tensed up. "Zey wonder where is team mascot. Has she been shot? Has she been killed? Srown in a river somewhere?

"But life goes on." He glanced at me, unseeing. "Soon as if little one never existing. Sandrine still spend all day under mosquito netting. She become hunched. She very thin. And her papa bury hisself in work, play market, move money. Do what it need to keep business running.

"Claude Ponsinet—big, young, handsome Kanak mine worker—come to house to talk business. Zen he visit Forestier house more often. More and more and more. Jacques like young man's company. Life begins to get better. Sandrine leave 'er bed. She walks about house again. She smile. She look happy.

"But soon Jacques gets big shock." The corners of Marcel's mouth twitched. "When he enters daughter's room wisout knocking, he find her wis Kanak. 'Off to Australia, monsieur,' he shout. 'You will work for me zere. It will be good job. Much money. You can 'ave anysing, but you cannot 'ave my daughter.'"

"What a bummer," I murmured. "Just when she was happy again."

"Well, Jacques Forestier 'ave business to run."

"What happened? Did Sandrine hate her father for mucking up her chance of happiness? Did she find someone else?"

"*Non*, she follow Claude."

"You mean Sandrine's *here*, living in Australia?"

"*Oui*, she somewhere in zis big country. She used to flirt at Papa, blow kisses. Now not ever talk, not write letter …" His voice trailed off.

"That so sucks," I said. "Because of her racist father, Sandrine's life went down the toilet."

We sat there in silence. The word 'toilet' began to intrude, making me think of the pee smell on Win, and on Namilly.

"Why, in your opinion, would a person suddenly, for the first time, like, ever, begin to smell of—*pee*?" I asked him.

Marcel's body jerked, as if startled. "*Pipi*? I 'ave no idea. Accident, per'aps?"

"And not only that, why would somebody bury jillions of perfume bottles in the garden?"

"Your muzzer? She is person who dig?"

"Yeah, she's the one I'm *really* worried about."

"I can see on 'er face she live with problem. She drink, maybe. She bury bottles from ze shame?"

I was shocked at the idea of Namilly guzzling perfume. "Well, she's got problems. But nobody in the world drinks perfume. That's so yuck!" I felt sick.

He shrugged. "Some people drink it. Not taste like wine, but work like wine. Alcohol is in perfume."

"No way." I shook my head. "Not Namilly." I thought for a bit. "Although there *is* the mumbling, the pee smell, the pushing her cans around in patterns. Bit odd, don't you think?" Marcel had come up with a strange solution to the mystery of the empty perfume bottles hidden beneath the canna patch.

"I feel better—well, sort of—for having discussed it. I'm not sure if you're right. Too off the planet. Well, I should get back to my V TRAMPS DREAM'N."

He raised an eyebrow.

"It's a mnemonic. Starts with *Venir*, then the other verbs follow. *Tomber*, to fall," I said, ticking them off with my fingers, "and so on. D'you see?"

I could see he didn't see.

"Well, I hope you manage to squirrel out Sandrine, and find her baby."

The wind had become icy. The sun was a low disc. Hugging my arms to my chest, I pushed along the shingles. My talk with Marcel had helped a bit, but I'd never thought anyone would sock down perfume. Certainly not Namilly.

As I climbed the cliff face, a thought hit me: Namilly drank her Sticky Berry dessert wine in front of me. Why would she swig bottles of Polka Dot scent in secret?

Chapter 17

Who would've dreamed a horse's bowel movements, in the greater scheme of things, could change your life?

I went to the house on Ti Point to speak to Marcel, find out if he had any other ideas about Namilly. I still found it hard to imagine her socking down perfume.

The curtains were drawn. Pine needles had built up on the doorstep. Orazio, the gardener, was buzzing around the lawn on his ride-on mower. Through a cloud of diesel fumes, I asked him if the Frenchman had left.

He said he thought he'd gone.

I trudged past Win's two-storey clapboard on my way home. I hadn't spoken to her since the incident on the Bay, but I could see her with Bill Einstein in the side paddock. Holding a garden hose, she was struggling to insert the plastic down his throat. Had she turned into a fruitcake? Become unhinged by her experience?

I kept walking. I had enough worries of my own.

"Hey, Gen, I need your help. C'mon, quick!" she called out.

I flirted with the idea of ignoring her.

"Jeez, I'm desperate. If you don't help he'll kick the bucket!"

I pushed the looped razor wire of the fence down with my thumb and forefinger, and stepped across. "What's up? I've got zilch time to muck around. I've got exams."

"Bill Einstein's constipated."

"So? Is that a big deal?"

"He'll die." Win's mouth was a thin line; her eyes vibrated with anguish. "His intestines'll swivel into big lumps with snaky bumps and knitted nodules. He'll lie down and it'll be the end, up shlep creek. And I can't *stand* the thought of being left with the paddle."

Her daggy plea had won me over. "I think you mean saddle," I murmured.

"Saddle?"

"You mean saddle, not paddle."

"Whatever. It's about full-on commitment." Her face was tight as she handed me the hose. "You can't let others take responsibility in this world."

"Yeah, yeah," I sighed. "What do I do?"

"I'll control the tap. You shove the water feature in his mouth. Don't worry if he jerks up. Be firm!" She was off, lecturing me in the way she had the night we sat beside the canna patch.

"Enough, okay? I still have to master the subjunctive. This exercise seems as iffy as my grammatical moods."

"Would you *like* to feed Bill Einstein to your *dog* for dinner?"

"Don't have a dog. But, if I did, I'd prefer not to feed him Bill Einstein. Ridgy-didge. He'd be too tough."

Her look was withering. She scurried to turn on the tap.

"Right, hose in?" she yelled.

I jabbed the jelly-shiny plastic towards Bill Einstein. His legs trembled. He lifted and rolled, as if he were standing on the high dive to hell. I wondered if his pins would break. That would *really* be the end then.

"Whoah, boy." I tried to make a sideways entry. The whites of his eyes began to boogie. I was imagining my arm in plaster, covered in autographs, my friends moving on to their affy year without me. Crushed by Bill Einstein.

"*Right*," screamed Win, "doing the big turn-on now."

The hose slid in nicely. Shot out again. Twisting from Bill Einstein's mouth, it swirled and swished across the ground until my T-shirt was drenched.

"Sex-eee," Win giggled. "Seriously, Gen. This is a life or death situation. Get it?"

"Got it!" I bellowed.

I thrust the hose in again. Bill Einstein rolled his eyes, belched, gulped the plastic. Gulped my finger, too.

"He got me!" I shrieked.

Blood coursed across my skin. The ground went spongy beneath me. The healing fluid flowed down his throat.

"OMG. Tetanus alert! You've had your shots?" squeaked Win.

"S'pose, when I was a baby."

My heart was pattering like the wings of Jack Bradfield's humungous moth in the moment before it was stabbed in the heart with a fat pin. And I still had all those verbs to finish. I'd be lolling in hospital in a coma for months on end, a massive sign erected on the highway: NO TOOTING PLEASE. And I'd be crazed with thirst, terrified of water.

"I've got rabies?" I quavered.

"Jeez, Gen. 'Course not. Not in this country. But we'd better get that wound cleaned. Then you can check your tetanus shots. Like to come in?"

Like to come in? Had Win said that? Was I about to become her *come-into-my-home* friend?

Now I'd see the inside of her house, see its goodies. Asian antiques. Porcelain from Paris. Christofle crystal. Conran couches. Wonderful Waterford. (All those fabbo things purchased by her mother, Alice Winstone, international editor of a fashion magazine.)

"Well," I murmured, feeling better already, "if you insist."

Chapter 18

Win's house was musty, which was understandable considering she lived mostly on her own.

In the entrance hall, against the wall, sat a trunk with frayed leather straps. An *antique*? Or just old?

The wax on the floor, built up darkly at the side of the passage, was worn to pale in the middle. The boards were cupped. My ankles wobbled as I walked. I collided with a horseshoe.

"You should hang this horseshoe curved upwards. If not, the luck'll fall out." I rubbed my foot with my uninjured hand.

Win seemed not to hear me.

I'd been expecting some sort of Aladdin's cave. On the other hand, I told myself, that trunk *could* be priceless, purchased at Sotheby's in New York by Alice with her paddle. I trailed behind Win, gazing at a bunch of framed bird prints. Mildew spattered, were they to die for? I was unable to tell.

My jaw dropped as we entered the poky room where Win cooked—worse than Namilly's sunroom kitchen. A bulb swayed from a frayed cord above a wooden table. Bentwood chairs, mismatched, sat randomly. The oven was chipped, coloured spew-green, with four sturdy legs and a black-knobbed door. Three burners were rusted, caked with grease, the fourth missing its parts. Curled signs on the cupboards: POTS, PLATES, MUGS, BEST PLATES, CUTLERY, GLASSES, CONTAINERS.

So *this* was the culinary engine room of the dwelling I'd always imagined as the glamorous *pied-à-terre* of a hip fashion writer. What a letdown. And why did Win need little notes to remind her of the contents of the cupboards?

She led me to the sink. The chrome on the taps was worn down to the brass—a black H in a white octagon on one faucet, C for cold indicator missing on the other. The latter's hole was filled with flyspecks.

She ran the water from the H tap, cold as a witch's elbow on my finger, pulled apart the skin to clean the wound. Her ice-blonde hair tumbled over her face as she worked. Her nose screwed into a neat ball.

I willed myself to resist dragging my finger away from her. I was determined not to die from any tetanus, rabies, or horrible horse flue.

"Cold flows from the hot tap, hot from the cold." She glanced up at me.

"Quaint," I said. "How's it look?"

"Not too bad. But you must be aware Bill Einstein is *not* the healthiest of people due to his advanced age. You should check those tetanus shots to be sure."

She drizzled methylated spirits over the area.

I skyrocketed towards the ceiling.

She ripped open a ratty Band-Aid with her teeth, and clamped it around my finger. I was clean, throbbing and, with a blinding flash, I remembered the last time I'd had my tetanus shot.

"It was when Namilly sliced off my toe," I cried.

"*What* was when she sliced off your toe?" Win looked startled.

"The vaccination."

"Should be okay, then. Like a drink?" She pressed the spring-loaded knob on the cupboard door, and whipped out two antique bottles of Coca Cola. Their crimped caps were corroded.

"I'm sure she did it on purpose."

"Did what, Gen?" Win pushed one bottle under the other, flicked off the lid, and handed me the bottle. The Coke was flat.

"Cut off my toe." I cogitated a bit. "Well, I'm sure she tried."

"Why'd she want to do a thing like that?"

"So she'd never have to go to the beach again."

"Well, she came for *me*—" The bottle was halfway to my lips when she snatched it from my hand, punched the crimped top back on, and opened her own bottle with a slick flick. Eased the lid off mine with her thumb, and handed it back.

"Yeah, she *did* come for you." I felt the green-eyed monster rear up again.

Win seemed uninterested in carrying on this tit-for-tat over Namilly's devotion. She stared at me stony-faced, a *time-to-get-outta-here* look. I gulped down the rest of my drink.

Turning to leave, I spied someone sitting in an armchair beyond the kitchen.

"That your mum?" But the woman's hair was mouse grey, coiled in matted springs about her head. Then I knew. "You've brought a Last Gasp Guesthouse guest into your house," I yelped. "From Grassberger's opposite? How grouse is that!"

Win nodded. "Yeah, gets pretty lonely here at times."

"Good for you!" I gave her the thumbs-up sign. "Life affirming to make friends with the wrinklies. All that wisdom and stuff."

I heard a voice croak, "Winnie, Winnie. Wee-wee. Wee-wee."

I froze. Last Gasp guests were never in such a bad way that they needed help in going to the toilet.

"Get out," Win hissed. "Leave!"

"Hey, hang on. *You* invited *me* in."

"Yeah, I should've let you die of tetanus." Her voice shook.

"I'm so *not* getting outta here 'til you tell me what's going on."

"Zip off!" She shoved me in the middle of my damp chest.

"You and whose army? I'm not leaving 'til you fill me in. What's that weirdo doing in your house?"

Win's eyes began to well up. Tears hovered on the edge of her lashes like an overfull saucepan. But I was determined to find out the identity of the woman with the toilet problem, who should learn a lesson or two from Bill Einstein, still calmly undergoing his colonic irrigation in the side paddock.

"It's my mum. Satisfied?" Her voice was soft.

My world began to fall about me in little lumps. "What about all those things you told me?" I was mind-blinded. "You *lied*."

"Don't come that one." A bubble of saliva burst with a snap on her lip. "I *never* lied. It was all in your imagination. She *does* go away. She disappears the *whole* time in her mind. And sometimes I can't *stand* it." (Was that the reason she had little content notes placed about the kitchen? For Alice's benefit?)

Win ran the back of her hand across her nose.

I went to her, put my arms around her.

"That bizzo with Bill Einstein," she whispered wetly into my neck, "hose down the throat—" Her breath was not so sweet that day.

"Yeah, what about the hose down the throat?" I pulled strands of hair from her face, tucked them behind her ear.

"Alice's Korsakoff's doctor told me how to do it." She burst into hacking sobs.

"Korsakov's? What the shivers is *that*?"

"Korsakoff! It's from the grog. You forget whole chunks of your life. You wet yourself."

"Well, her doctor's sure ace at getting body fluids moving."

Win continued to sob until I thought her heart would break.

"C'mon, show me," I murmured. "I haven't laid eyes on your mum since I was a little tacker. Could help, you know, help her remember. I can study later."

My knees felt like butter. What the hell was Korsakoff's?

Chapter 19

Win's show and tell was ghastly. Worse than those icky ones back in Grade 6. (Angela's mum's menstrual-stained knickers, Hetty's dad's pubic hairs in a plastic bag, six of Stefan's sun scabs spread in a circle on a white tissue.) Hers was far more gut-wrenching. A prize for awfulness? She would've won hands down. I was ashamed I'd never guessed.

But—Korsakoff's? I'd never even *heard* of that disease.

I trailed behind her into the dim room which had probably been a sunroom like ours, before Namilly decided to turn it into a kitchen. (Were sunless sunrooms an expression of hope in a windswept place?) I could smell pee and steamed pumpkin. Everything became clear. Win's story about feeding bubble and squeak to Bill Einstein? *She'd meant her mother.*

The gag from the smell slipped back down my throat.

A television flickered station identification in the corner. Alice Winstone's blank gaze was fixed on the screen. A smile was on her lips. Her eyes were empty. The nappy-changing moment seemed to have slipped her mind.

"She likes to have her hair brushed," Win whispered.

I pointed to the matted locks.

"Not combed. She screams, pushes me away," Win sniffed, "weeps when she doesn't like what I cook. But if she doesn't eat she'll die."

"You'd be free then, of whatever it is she's got."

"What an *awful* thing to say," she hissed. "She's my *mother*, for Chrissake!"

"Sorry, it slipped out. Anyway, you're lucky."

"Lucky?" Her voice was bitter.

"You know who your mother is."

"Yeah, s'pose. The booze brought it on, but."

"Brought on the what? The Korsakov's thingummy?"

"Korsakoff's *Syndrome.* Yeah, it does that, causes it."

"Your dad in China? Or d'you make that up, too?" It was obvious I'd had no idea what went on inside her house.

"Dunno anymore. He had a good job, though. Then he left, 'cos of the grog." She gave me a sideways look. "And 'cos of—"

"'Cos of what? Her grog problem wasn't reason enough?"

Win took a breath. "I'll tell you one day, not yet."

"When?"

"When you find your birth mother."

"But I might never find my birth mother. I've left my name on half a dozen websites, chat rooms, Human Services." I screwed up my brow. "Nothing."

"Maybe your mother's looking for *you*. Had you thought of that?"

"Hellooo." A voice came from the depths of the armchair. "Are you Chinese?"

"Hey, remember me?" I gave Alice a little wave. "No way am I Chinese. Why?"

She pointed at my plait. A trickle of vomit dangled from the corner of her lip.

"Sorreee. It's more, sort of, like—um—French." I felt a dork making conversation with someone who spent her time off the air. I'd never been good with the handicapped, apart from Stefan.

"Ohhh." Her voice descended to a stage whisper. "I used to have a daughter like you. She went away a long time ago. She was Chinese, too."

"Cripes," muttered Win, "most she's said in a month."

My friend's show and tell was apparently meant to stay silent.

"Nurse here," Alice said, jabbing a finger at Win, "doesn't understand. My daughter was a beautiful girl."

"Still is." I placed my arm around Win's shoulder.

Alice Winstone lost interest in our conversation. She bleared at the blinking television.

"Does she walk?" I looked at Win.

"She's not *paralysed*," she snapped. "And she didn't mistake you for a hat. Sideshow's over, you can go now." She led me to the front door.

"You *did* try to end it on the Bay, didn't you?"

She didn't reply. Her violet eyes were dull.

The key turned in the lock behind me. As my lungs gorged on clean sea air, Bill Einstein gave a multi-mega fart. A vast yellow stream erupted, swooshed, cascaded to the ground. He yawned. The hose fell from his mouth, jerked and sprayed and narrowly missed the steaming heap.

I gazed at the manure, a golden pile, a sunny pile, a hill of hope, and laughed. Life was not so bad, after all.

"She's in a bad mood again, but she'll be out to give you an elephant stamp." I rubbed his nose. His body shivered.

I hurried off to go over a few equations for my maths exam the next day, and maybe get together with those iffy subjunctives.

Korsakoff's? If I went online, would Jules be there to unload on? Would he be able to fill me in on that disease?

Chapter 20

"Come here." She puts her arms around my friend, and comforts her.

"I brought you manure," Win whispers, "but there's a hole in my bucket. It's run down my leg."

"Mustn't let your pretty head worry about the slightest thing. I will protect you. One small chore. Dole the manure out in piles around the garden, then take these flowers. They'll do the job."

I swam up from the dream.

I leapt out of bed. Through the window, I saw Namilly pushing flowers into Win's arms. Yellow narcissus. Dahlias of every hue. Sprigs of mauve tubular salvia.

Win buried her nose in the blooms. She marched off past the grevillea cubby. The gate clanged shut behind her.

Why was Namilly giving Win flowers?

Motes hung suspended in the morning air. Cannas frizzled their reflection in the bedroom mirror. I rubbed my eyes, glanced at my watch.

Heck, I had a Maths in Space exam that morning, in less than an hour. I'd riffled through a few algebraic equations the night before, enough to get me up to speed. But I'd been bothered by Win, bothered by her mother's illness.

Although, it was the French oral that had me packing the most. I could hardly think about it without my heart flipping from the high dive. Maths over, I'd hunker down with my verbs again.

I feverishly hauled up my jeans. No time to check my emails. No time to meet Jules, who had not been in the chat room when I logged on the previous night. I flew out the door. I'd be forced to walk the long way, using Ravella Crescent. I couldn't risk bumping into the bogans, I told myself.

I snatched a banana passionfruit from the vine for breakfast, touched its creamy surface three times for luck. Split it with my thumbnail.

A smell erupted, as if the septic tank beneath the canna patch had exploded during the night and painted the creeper with excrement. I eyed the fruit. Sniffed. It seemed okay.

The smell rose up, and I looked down. That stink had come from the garden bed. A golden heap of horse manure sat beside my feet.

So, I hadn't dreamt it when Namilly told Win she'd protect her. And that bunch of flowers she gave her? What was going on?

Chapter 21

Stefan and I joined up after the maths exam. We jostled our way out of Ravella Community Hall together. As the bus shook its way back to The Store, we sat in silence, wrung out from too much thinking.

He pulled a fat tube of SPF 30+ from his pocket when we alighted, applied it in gross heaps. Smoothed it, until he began to look like a figure in a snow dome.

"Skye said you went in," he said.

"Went in where?"

"Win's." His pale eyes peered at me through a mountain of face protection.

"A snake in the grass at Grassberger's? A spy in our midst?"

"Seriously, mate, what's it like?" Apparently I wasn't the only person consumed with curiosity about Win Winstone.

"S'okay." I gave a nonchalant shrug. I wasn't about to tell him it was the absolute pits. Most people wouldn't deign to cross the threshold if they knew what was in there. But I intended to guard Win's secret like a sacred trust.

"Her ma there?"

"Yeah."

"Good sort? Like Win?" Did Stefan lie in bed at night mentally perving on my friend?

I looked at him. He grinned. His teeth were yellow against the white of the zinc cream. Nope, he was joshing. And I had his letter to prove it.

"About your letter—"

But he hadn't finished with his interrogation. "She normal, like Jane?" (Jane Becker was a flibbertigibbet sort of female.)

"Why d'you think she isn't normal?" Did Stefan know about Alice's condition? "Naw, she's zonked from travelling. Bit off the air, that's all."

"Be gone again soon?"

"What's with the questions?" I was finding it hard to lie like this. "I'm sure she's left already." How did Win do it all the time? Then again, she didn't lie. Just dropped hints, answered questions with questions.

I decided to change the subject. "Win flicks caps off bottles, just by using other bottles."

"Why not use an opener, or the ring pull?"

Stefan's question stumped me. We lapsed into silence.

He kicked up loose dirt on the side of the road. His ears began to turn pink in the sun. I saw a new lesion on his left lobe, which he'd missed with the SPF 30+, oozing gently. I felt an urge to touch it, discover what it felt like.

Was Stefan's problem more than sun allergy laced with a bit of end-stage acne? Was he facing the onset of serious psoriasis? If so, his life would be difficult. (He'd never be able to adopt a baby; those ernie agencies wouldn't like it at all.)

"Why'd she bother to do that?"

"I dunno. Put a sock in it, Stef. You sound like a three-year-old."

"Vince warned me." He shoved a freckled finger in my face.

"About what? Girls in general? Or just me?" If he didn't watch it, I'd return his eternity proposal posthaste. "Anyway, your father should know."

"Why?"

"There you go again with the 'why' word. Vince's famous."

"For what?"

"Knocking off the cashier chicks, the ones with the big knockers. Pardon the pun."

"Oh, get fucked!" He stormed off, cut through the ti-trees and disappeared.

I didn't feel guilty. At least Stefan *had* a father.

Stuffed from too much maths, I pushed open the cyclone wire gate. The exam had been okay, but I'd found it hard to concentrate. All that business with Win while I was kept in the dark freaked me out.

To make matters worse, Angela Rasmussen'd giggled her way through a whole set of mathematical equations as if they were the funniest things she'd seen in her entire life. Her springy dark hair flew all over the place. From the back of the room, Jason barely took his eyes off her. Was my book wrecking his chance of a good career?

Hetty Geiger, in her megaton geek glasses, Indian plaits lank upon her shoulders—totally unlike the panache of my French one—and her clothes reeking of tobacco, had whispered as we filed into the hall that she'd seen Jack Bradfield zipping up his trousers as he scrambled from her window—a quantum leap from only looking. "Yeah?" I'd said. But I wasn't sure whether to believe her. Perhaps she'd spiked her chop-chop. Or was off the planet from too much book bashing.

Stefan had chewed his fingernails for three hours, pondered a lot, scratched a scab from his face and rolled it into a ball with his thumb and forefinger as he gazed out the window. Gross!

Win, older than the rest of us, had only two subjects to sit: British History—I'd seen her sweating over the Corn Laws—and Biology, before she moved on to her affy year. Would she go up to the city with its skyscrapers and perpetual rain? Or stay in Ravella and look after Alice?

I pulled the mail from the letterbox. Only one letter, addressed to me, was postmarked Cannes. *Snail mail from France*? It seemed the search for my birth mother was bearing fruit.

I ripped the envelope open to find it had nothing to do with my birth parents. The letter was from Marcel:

Dear Genna, he wrote. *I is in place with palm trees and tropical rain. I feel much at home. There is many coconuts.*

Odd. I had no idea Cannes was so humid.

I examined the franking of the envelope closely. Cairns. I decided to check my emails before reading what he had to say.

I booted up. The screen was still wavy, the words like Chinese characters in a rainstorm. I needed a new screen, but didn't have the cash.

Being paid to clip box plants and stock the woodpile didn't provide nearly enough dough. Losing a hundred bucks didn't help, either. I'd be forced to wait until after my exams, when Arch Biddle went on leave and I did shelf-stacking at The Store. I went to my letterbox.

Checking mail … Receiving mail …

I was bumped by the server. Asked if I wished to reconnect, I punched Enter. A ton of spam. I pressed the Delete button, consigned it to the rubbish bin.

One message was left. From Marcel: *I am sending letter in pos*t.

Apparently Marcel had discovered my email address? Had he done so on a birth search website? He seemed to be finding out more and more about me.

Chapter 22

Marcel was beginning to give me the willies. What did he want with me? I needed something to sustain me before I read his letter.

I jammed the juicer together, reflecting that in comparison to Win's my cuisine was terribly haute, donned my safety specs and chopped. Three non-genetically-modified carrots for my vision went down the feed chute. A chunk of crisp cauliflower for my bowels. Macrobiotic ginger to make my blood flow. Breaking my raw vegan diet, I popped in a dried anchovy for brain food.

The machine spewed ochre fluid into the glass. Particles of vegetables hung in the air as I swigged.

I grabbed an organic apple, a handful of sundried raisins from a Tupperware container marked *Raisins Secs* and retired to the hollow sofa with Marcel's closely written sheets.

In a mixture of English and French, a sort of franglais, he wrote about the woman he'd spoken of on the rocks, Sandrine Bas Salaire de Lyon.

It was obvious that reading it would not be a waste of time. It would help me with my studies. I began to gobble up his letter.

Sandrine arrive in Cairns. She hurry down East Coast of Australia to find her new lover, Claude Ponsinet—he make her feel alive as

Yves-Laurent have done. She search streets of Runaway Bay. Nobody ever hear of big Kanak mine worker. So she fill in time by buying all sorts of chic things, Gucci, Chanel and other nice brands, by using her Carte Bleue. (Carte Bleue is best card in world!) She still feel a despair, though. Bronzing herself on beach one day, she sees well-muscled lifesaver. Todd's muscles are like big, big mountains.

Marcel's descriptions of Sandrine's affair with her lifesaver seemed unnecessary from a man I barely knew. *Chat*? What did that have to do with anything? I shouldn't have been reading this. I definitely needed *Merde! The French Your Teachers Never Taught You.* These descriptions were way too florid.

I began to feel edgy. Were these details a come-on from this man? Why was he unloading on me, telling me about this stranger's issues? I'd heard warnings about the net, paedophiles in chat rooms.

Was Marcel a sleazy internet stalker? If so, I should install a firewall. Get a MailMarshal.

More importantly, was he planning to come back and *do* something? What was he after? Money? I was broke until Arch Biddle went on holidays.

I bit into my apple and read on:

Sandrine feel guilty when she think about her daughter. Was she safe, back in Nouméa? She place collect call to Jacques Forestier who is charmed to hear from her. She say she's been busy. This is reason she not in touch. Jacques tell her he know everything is well by Carte Bleue. Her credit card is like blue postcard. It arrive every four weeks. From card, he know where she is, how much she spend. No need for her to bother her beautiful head about a thing. Sandrine then ask about *Nounou* and Geneviève …

The pages slid from my fingers. Sandrine's daughter's name was Geneviève? My head began to spin. I remembered Marcel quizzing me about my name. Was any of this to do with having left my details on the website? Was it a devious method for him to worm into my life?

I crammed the remainder of the raisins into my mouth, ploughed on:

Jacques Forestier say *Nounou* and Geneviève with her. So perhaps she can tell him about them.

Sandrine reply that she not see them for several days. She wonder if they return to Nouméa. Jacques comfort her, say *Nounou* must have taken child to visit friends. He is sure nanny will be in touch soon. He say life still hard on island, fighting still going on. His office is damaged by car bomb.

Sandrine is very worried. How long since anyone has seen Geneviève and *Nounou*?

She know she cannot go home. Jacques Forestier can forgive most things, like loss of mine skip, plunge of Bourse. But never ever losing his beautiful grandchild. She decide to stay put. She find work in shop that sell swimming costume while she search for Geneviève. She have big problems. Schoolies week remind her of home, with students' hairs in dreadlocks. Rapping. Hip-hop.

But one happy day, she see her lover. Claude walk past Carole's Cossies (bloody awful name!) as she sweep sand from shop. Not too much of a coincidence. For Gold Coast is like suburb of Nouméa!

I put down the pages. This story was turning into a saga. I needed a break. I eased myself off the brick-like hollow sofa. I stuffed the pages I'd read into an old pair of joggers in my bedroom cupboard, and pushed the unread ones into the back pocket of my jeans. I peered through the topiary box plants into the garden. No Namilly. I recalled that bizzo with the flowers. Was she with Win right now?

Chapter 23

I knocked at Win's front door, in a bit of a dither now I knew about Alice's strange disease. No answer. No sign of Namilly. I decided to continue on to the beach, read the remainder of the letter there, and clear the cobwebs from my head at the same time.

Beneath the overhang of the cliff I chose a flat stone and settled myself alongside The Cauldron. The wind was churning an ominous swell. I needed to finish this quickly, move on to the future perfect tense waiting at my desk.

> Claude involve himself in her business. White shoes, rainbow lorikeet on his shoulder to remind him of home, he meet friends each day for coffee at Tedder—chic place. He decide to buy out Carole, run boutique with Sandrine. She tells her father of her plans. (But not about Claude being with her.) *Ravi*, he load up her Carte Bleue by electronic transfer. Then he ask after health of *Nounou* and Geneviève. Sandrine is scared, she pray Jacques Forestier never find out the truth.
>
> Carole's Cossies take off in hot-pink theme. Free from worries about independence movement—

I paused. We'd studied that at school: the dreads, the rasta, the rifles. Cool.

Sandrine feel as if she is back at Anse Vata beach now, happy. And business briefly boom. But her papa spoil things for her by requesting photos of baby granddaughter. Did baby granddaughter look like him? Sandrine is unable to sleep at night thinking about it. And Claude fret much about her health in the head.

She worry about how she will obtain snaps of her daughter. Pushing her hangers on the rack like abacus, she work out Geneviève must be seven years old by now. At least.

She place ads in local paper, full page ones which cost much. Her heart go fast each time she receive a letter of her papa. It always same, he is saying: 'I want snaps of Geneviève!'

I nibbled on a nail. Why was Marcel telling me these things?

Every evening Sandrine return, very unhappy, to her pink house in Cockleshell Court—water frontage, Mustang boat moored to jetty at bottom of garden (that boat cost big, big money).

Soon business begin to suffer. Many expenses: florist bills, Claude's teeth, birdseed for rainbow lorikeet, dry cleaning for Claude's shirts, damaged clothing from bloody schoolies week.

Sandrine cannot imagine what her daughter look like anymore. She cannot imagine her little face. But she think Geneviève should have blonde hairs like hers, same blue eyes, skin same. She will not resemble her father—handsome, dark man. For z'oreille soldier not make pretty girl!

Sandrine imagine her daughter still wear white dresses with ribbons, flowers in blonde hairs. She crazy lady. She begin to stop young girls in long dresses, ask if name is Geneviève. And girls don't like this. Jacques Forestier is more impatient by each letter. 'WHERE ARE THE PHOTOS?' he is saying. 'Is she like me?' he ask.

The waves heaved and smashed over The Cauldron, as impatient as any old man. I placed the pages I'd read on a flat rock beside me, struck by the similarity. *Are you sure your name is not Geneviève?*

What a loony way to locate a missing person. There must be more scientific methods: births, deaths, marriages, health department, taxation, customs, hospital lists, rent records, real estate sales, credit cards. And, of course, the internet. Not available then, but all the go today.

Was Marcel looking for Geneviève on Sandrine's behalf? Jacques Forestier's? Or did he just like checking out chicks he'd come across in cyberspace? Was it a ruse to get closer to me?

I pushed loose bits of hair from my eyes, and decided to wade through the remainder of this mega epistle.

Chapter 24

I couldn't wait to find out how Marcel's story ended. Had Sandrine wormed her way out of this situation with her father? Snaps of a non-existent Geneviève were too far out. What a mess this chick'd got herself into.

Waves were whipping up, the clouds closing in. I was hooked on his tale.

Pleasant event happen. A family move into next door house in Cockleshell Court, a couple with daughter. Matilda not beautiful like Geneviève. But she of similar years in her age. Sandrine decide girl will make good model for her photographs. She plan to get to know her.

Matilda wear glasses and ugly jeans. Her hairs is tied back with elastic. But she can make good (in nice robe, from distance!) baby Geneviève. Sandrine persuade her to put on best dress, let her hairs hang down, tie on side with ribbons she provide. (Frock ugly, but what can you do?)

Matilda pose hand on hip. She pose on jetty. Pose sitting in Mustang boat. Pose doing handstand, somersault, skip. Then fall in water and ribbons shrink. But, voilà, Sandrine have what she want—*snaps for Papa!*

My eyes were on stalks. Taking fake photos? How bad was that?

Jacques Forestier much excited. He think Geneviève resemble his side of family, height *incroyable* for her age. Her hairs is darker than he remember. Were genes of great-grandmother coming out? Can Sandrine send more photos, please?

Sandrine promise to send more when camera, hit to ground by model during parade, is fixed. She lies. Lately, there is no parade. But she need time to arrange different clothing. Elegant, white, made of lovely lace.

Was this bird nuts? *Nobody* wore loserish white lace dresses. Except, maybe, Elizabeth.

Jacques Forestier make Sandrine nervous. He ask about *Nounou*, suggest she send snaps of Geneviève and *Nounou* together. Sandrine say she will do this when next she have free weekend. She is busy. It is raining. She will do it when sun shines again.

About to hang up, she hear her papa say he will come to Australia to see his beautiful daughter and wonderful granddaughter. Business permitting! Sandrine sink to floor and cry and cry.

(And still Jacques not know about Claude, who is standing next to her.)

But Papa too busy. Important Kanak leader shot dead. Road to Tontouta airport cut off.

Sandrine is safe. For the moment. She arrange to meet mother of Matilda, a lady called Colette. She persuade her to be *Nounou* in photos without telling her the reason. With Matilda on ground beside her mother, she has perfect pictures of *Nounou* and Geneviève. Very naughty, eh?

'Very naughty, eh?' More like the total *pits*. I gnawed on my nails.

Jacques Forestier write. He is very happy. He say *Nounou* thinner than he remember. Younger, too. It must be the surf—no surf in Nouvelle-Calédonie, only lagoon.

Sandrine work hard in shop. She ask Claude to ask Carole to sell her final share of boutique. Then she make everything in pink. Mainly monokini. (No top of bathing costume, you understand?!)

Mmmn. *'No top of bathing costume, you understand?!'* Was this *the come-on*?

One day, Jacques Forestier turn up in Australia. He ring Sandrine from Coolangatta airport. Say he is coming to visit her, see his granddaughter. (He also look very much forward to seeing *Nounou*!) This is last conversation he will ever have with Sandrine. When he arrive at shop, it is locked. So he drive to house in Cockleshell Court, also empty. He see girl skipping on footpath. She is same as girl in photos. He know he has been tricked. And it break up his heart.

I placed the letter carefully on the boulder beside me, horrified by Sandrine Bas Salaire de Lyon's actions. What a stone-heart! What a screwed-up bird! Was she still hiding from her father? What a tacky thing to do, sending those fake photos. Then again, she was in love with Claude.

I was torn by this tale, a love story with a twist about two people who, in the normal scheme of things, would never have been together. Had their relationship survived? I imagined so. If not, airhead Sandrine would've returned to Noumea, begged her father's forgiveness, and searched for her daughter in a logical manner.

Why had Marcel put all this in writing? I found this letter thing spooky. Anyway, what was he doing in Cairns? Looking for Geneviève? Decided to fill me in *just in case* I was *wondering*? This was shaping up as a weirdo form of net stalking. I should probably warn Namilly, in case he *did* something.

The pine trees surrounding the house on Ti Point soughed gently. An eerie sound, it made me think of my birth mother. Was she looking down on me? Would I ever find out about her?

I reached for the pages, planning to put them with the others hidden in my joggers, but the wind snatched them from my fingers. They swooped and soared as I leapt to grab them, flicked and floated on the air currents, wheeled across the waves. Subsided. Sank at the spot where Win had been blown in her rubber dinghy.

I trudged up the path from the beach, back to my own reality. Namilly and her hollow sofa and hospital whiff. Win and her sweet breath and Alice's illness. Stefan and his blue ringers, shells and written declarations.

And, if I didn't study soon, my ENTER scores would get me nowhere.

Chapter 25

I decided not to tell Namilly about Marcel's letter. She'd say it was my fault for wasting time in chat rooms. But I found it hard to concentrate. His story was messing with me. Was it a kinky get-on? A sinister plot of some sort? I needed to go online. I booted up, typed in *www.babesinwoods.com*.

Jules took my mind off things. Again, he commented on how much we had in common. Told me not to worry. I signed off, and went to my letterbox.

Checking mail … Receiving mail … One message: *À bientôt, Marcel.*

So, Marcel planned to see me soon. My heart began to thud. This guy was definitely a stalker.

A rap at the door. Namilly stood there clutching flowers.

"I'm studying." My eyes fixed on the convolvulus and salvia, the golden balls, purple tubular leaves. A heady smell.

"Could you take these to Win? She knows what to do with them."

I hesitated. What did one normally *do* with a bunch of flowers? Shove them in water and enjoy the aroma. With that pee smell, the odour of boiled cabbage and steamed pumpkin, it seemed hardly worth the effort. Namilly's eyes appeared to glisten as I took them from her.

She turned on her heel and marched off, the boards of the passage shaking beneath her step.

Why had she not given the flowers to Win herself? How much did she actually know about Alice? (There'd been no answer when I knocked to see if Namilly was there, before I made my way to the beach to finish reading the letter.) I wasn't sure she knew anything at all about Alice Winstone.

I gave my hair a quick brush, and gathered it into a loose ponytail. Deciding to change into my joggers, I reached inside to pull out the pages of Marcel's letter and discovered the shoe was empty. I loosened the laces, tipped each shoe upside down and shook. They were definitely not there. Had Namilly been snooping?

I marched into the garden, flowers flopping in my face. Namilly was clipping dead heads off the daisies near the grevillea cubby when I charged up to her.

"Where is my letter?" I was peed off. "The one from Monsieur Manet."

"I buried it, or what there was of it."

I sucked back my breath at her honesty. "How *dare* you. It was *mine*."

"The words were obscene." She continued clipping.

"How do you know?"

"I read them. I imagine you binned the rest?"

"It was *my* letter. And *where* did you bury it? With the …" I bit my tongue, having almost spilled the beans about the perfume bottles I'd unearthed beneath the canna patch.

"Under the Norfolk Island tree with Serge Gainsbourg … they deserve each other." Her sniff was a snort. She continued to snip the last of the blooms. "Win rode by on Bill Einstein this morning. Had she no exam?"

"She's completed maths."

"Lucky she didn't kill the nag! He'll be off to the knackery any day now!" Namilly retrieved the shears at her feet, and began to shape the grevillea cubby.

I slammed the gate behind me, shirty that she'd buried my letter. I was so wild I could feel steam chugging out my ears. And now I'd have to face Win.

Would Win be aggro that I'd found out about Alice? Would things have changed between us? I was toey.

Chapter 26

The blinds of the two-storey clapboard were drawn. The Winstone house had an eerie, quiet feel, an air of emptiness and bubbled paint. Cicadas buzzed fitfully. Started up here. Stopped there. Began somewhere else.

I knocked. Bill Einstein grazed in the side paddock. He seemed in good nick after having Win on his back that morning. His ribs were like mountain chains, but he didn't appear to be ready for the knackery just yet.

The deadlock turned. The door groaned open. Win was barefoot, her cut-offs covered in grimy spots. Not a flicker of friendliness showed on her face.

"Yeah?" Her gaze took in the flowers.

"Namilly asked me to give you these." I shoved the bunch at her. "She said you'd know what to do with them. Whatever *that* means."

Win's eyes were glazed. Her breath was sugary. Her nail polish was chipped. She'd fallen a long way from her previous immaculate self.

"You gonna take 'em or not?"

"The old bag in the back won't care. It's a waste of time, doesn't help at all."

"What do you mean, doesn't help? How could a bunch of flowers help?"

"With memory loss. It's an old wives' tale about the plants. She pushes it, but it doesn't work." She sniffed. "*Nothing* works."

"Who pushes it?"

"Your mother, Namilly."

Apparently Namilly was more up to speed with the Winstone situation than I'd realised. Then I remembered her whispering in Win's ear on the day she was blown out on the Bay.

"Frankly, I don't care what either of you thinks about these stupid flowers." I thrust them into her hands. No way was I taking them back home to face the inevitable inquisition.

Win rattled her keys in the deadlock, as if to close the door. Then paused. "Come in, say hello to the bitch."

Her mood swing was suss, and she looked stoned. But I was dying to see the inside of her house again.

"Give 'em to Alice yourself." She shoved the flowers back at me, strode off snapping, "She's out back in the same stinking chair."

I passed the leather trunk, sidestepped the horseshoe still lying on the floor, and found Alice in her armchair. Her locks were more knotted and springy than ever. The television flashed in the corner, reflecting a kaleidoscope of colour on the opposite wall. I was surprised she didn't go ape with migraines. A cabbage stink fought with the smell of pumpkin mash. An odour of pee filled the atmosphere. I began to feel woozy.

"Sure the television's not bothering you?" I yelled, as though English was her second language.

She stayed mute. Dorothy danced along the Yellow Brick Road with her friends. I picked up the remote, flicked the channel to SBS for something quieter. A French film. A bald guy and his girlfriend were naked on a table. Uh-oh. *How so embarrassing.*

Feeling hot, I hastily changed the channel back. Alice didn't seem to notice. I held out the flowers. She frisked her head away.

I was wasting my time, I decided. I should leave Namilly's offering on the floor, go home to my conditional perfect.

"Helloooo." A trembling voice floated its way up from the depths of the armchair. "Do you get *60 Minutes*?"

Her question was clear, if a bit off-beam. Everyone in the world received *60 Minutes*.

"Yeah, and we have a satellite dish on our roof, so we get all sorts of transmissions."

She wasn't interested in my viewing habits. "You're the Chinese girl." She pointed. "I like your plait."

My hair wasn't in a plait, but we were making progress. She'd recognised me, at last. Was the scent of salvia chasing away her Korsakoff thingamajig? I offered her the bunch again.

This time, she grasped it with trembling fingers and buried her nose in the blooms. If I concentrated hard, I could see she'd been ace looking in her day.

"Grouse of you." I smiled, thinking it never hurt to be polite.

One of the mismatched bentwood chairs had escaped from the kitchen. I dragged it towards me, and sat down cautiously.

"Can I put them in water for you?"

Alice continued to hang on to the flowers for dear life. She was strangling the stems as if they were a lifeline to somewhere, a better place with no memory lapses.

"What did you do today?" I was sure she'd done nothing at all.

"I went down to the beach, gathered seashells," she replied in a wobbly, whispery voice.

"Did you go on your own?"

"Where did I go on my own?" Her eyes were interested.

"To the beach."

"Did I?"

"Yeah, you just told me. But did you go on your own?"

"Go where?"

"To the beach."

"How nice. Did you go to the beach, too?" she asked.

Win said her mother rarely spoke, I could see she'd been holding this in for a long, long while.

"What's your name, dear?"

I was about to tell her I was Alice and she was Genna when I heard a click from the vicinity of the kitchen. Win waved a metal nozzle, and made a pumping motion with a lever behind a cylinder.

PUMP. PUMP. PHSST. PHSST. A blue flame shot out of the blowtorch.

"What *do* you think you're doing?" I tried to sound calm.

The blowtorch glistened as she aimed it in my direction. Win looked far less balanced than her mum, seated in her armchair beside me, smiling, sniffing, and humming tunelessly in a high-pitched quaver while she shredded leaves upon her knee.

The room seemed brighter than a photographic studio. My T-shirt began to stick to my armpits as though I'd used Super Glue for deodorant. There was a tight band around my chest. What did Win plan to do? Give me a heat-treated facelift? Scar me forever?

I took a deep breath. "And what do you think you are *doing*?" I repeated, my voice cracking on the upturn.

"Don't worry dear, she does this all the time," Alice mumbled from the depths of her smelly seat.

Win, eyes glassy, jerked her head at the kitchen, indicating I should follow.

"I'd go back to China, dear," Alice announced from the safety of her padding.

I rose from the bentwood chair and followed my friend to the room with the single dangling bulb, and the old stove where she manufactured her slops with goo caked upon its surrounds.

I pointed to the door. "There's a sign missing. You should have OVEN written there."

"Cut the cracks," she said.

"Put that thing *down*, you cretin," I hissed. "You're behaving in a very iffy manner."

"Start cooking the dinner."

"Whaddya mean 'start cooking the dinner'?"

Win wagged a digit at the vegetables on the draining board. Green eyes stared from the coat of a potato. Fleurettes of a piece of limp broccoli were crowned with yellow. A quarter of cabbage had black mould along its spine. I could see no meat, no protein at all. Had Win become a vegan, too?

"If you get on so well with the old bag, you can start chopping. I've had enough of mopping spew, spooning food, wiping arse, combing knots from her ugly dreads. It's *your* turn now. See how *you* like it."

"Dream on, kiddo."

PUMP. PUMP. PHSST. PHSST. I backed off as the blue flame from her blowtorch shot towards me.

Three battered triangular saucepans sat in a circle, like a cake cut in three slices, a sort of sponge of saucepans. A loose handle sat beside the burners, ready to be slotted through a soldered loop. (Had they been baby-proof pots for Win, now turned oldie-proof pots for Alice?)

I was not in the mood to have my face rearranged, so I began to chop the vegetables. *Should I try to stab my friend in the stomach? Make a run for it?* I wondered. Then again, knowing my luck, I'd misjudge and end up with third degree burns. Best to play along with her, continue with my task, I decided.

"I said I'd get water for Alice's flowers." I spoke in a soothing, placatory voice. "Anyway, there's no protein. She needs nuts."

"Needs nuts? She *is* nuts." Win made a crooning noise, and began to waltz around the kitchen cradling her blowtorch. "Just chop and boil. You can load up the washing machine next."

Chapter 27

The vegetables simmered in their battered pots. Win pumped her blowtorch in my direction. PUMP. PHSST. A burst of flame.

I scampered up the stairs.

"Strip Alice's bed!"

Alice's room was a mess. This hassle city with her mother was getting to Win, and I couldn't say I blamed her. I tried to hang tough, as though I'd been doing this all my life, briefly wondering how Skye Becker coped at Grassberger's Guesthouse. However, Last Gasp guests were not ill. And their pockets were lined with dosh to dull the pain.

I cupped my hand over my mouth to hide the gag. Win was unfazed. Her nose didn't even twitch. But she lived with horrors I could only imagine.

I wiped my lips with the back of my hand, gathered up the sheets and dumped them atop a heap of dirty T-shirts lying on her bedroom floor.

The walls of Win's room, once powder blue, were smudged and faded. Swags, stained from the salty mist that seeped up from Port Phillip Bay and crept across the windowsill, drooped limply. So much for my dreams about Alice, international fashion editor.

Blowtorch pointed, Win picked up a tiny bottle with her free hand from the kidney dressing table. She unscrewed the cap with her teeth, spat out the plastic and swigged.

I sucked in my breath at the sight of the label: Polka Dot.

The words glowed and spat like a neon sign as I had another mind-blinding moment. Namilly wasn't drinking the perfume. It was Win. Her sweet breath? She wasn't diabetic at all. She was socking down scent.

"What're you *doing*?" I squeaked.

She bleared in my direction. "What's it look like?"

"It's disgusting to drink perfume. Yucky." I could feel my insides squirm.

"You should talk. You're into that weirdo raw veg thing. You could get crypto—" Her voice trailed away.

"—sporidium? That's different. And I wash my hands. Look, smoke chop-chop if you need something. At least it's healthier."

"No buzz in chop-chop, Gen." She looked confused. "It's the flowers does it."

"What's the flowers?"

"They're good for you." Win pointed to the bottle in her hand. "Cure all sorts of things, like, when I'm down. Could also stop me getting Korsakoff's." (She'd certainly changed *her* tune about the medicinal value of flowers.)

"In your dreams. It's grog, you idiot. Marcel said. And *not* the sort you're meant to swallow."

"*What's* grog? And who's Marcel? That creep hanging around on the beach?"

"He's a Caldoche. And he said they use alcohol when they make the scent."

"No, they don't, they only use flowers. Anyway, they say you've gotta get worse before you get better."

"Where'd you get those bottles from?" My face grew stern. "They don't come cheap, except maybe Polka Dot."

"Namilly."

"My mum's your supplier?" My world was slipping away.

"Yeah. She gets 'em from Mrs B at the Zabaglione Woollen Shop, gives 'em as gifts to make me feel okay. Dirt cheap, she says, cheaper than chop-chop. And none of that bleach to bust your brains, turn your lungs to mush, send you screaming into space."

I had another epiphany, my third in the last few days. It was becoming clear: Namilly had been burying perfume bottles to protect Win. But from whom? The garbos? I was so out of the loop.

"The bottles, the ones I found," I stuttered, "in the canna patch, that night?"

"What bottles in the canna patch?"

"I dug some up."

"I won't even *bother* to ask why you were scrounging around in there. *Grossss*," she slurred.

"Namilly's been burying 'em. Not as obvious as heaving them over the fence with her cans, I s'pose. Not that anybody looks. The flies are putrefaction enough to keep people away. Does she actually know what you're doing with the scent?"

Win licked her lips.

"Anyway, why would she, like, *help* you, if help is the right word? AA would be more appropriate."

"Because SHE is the reason my father left." Her eyeballs raked the room. "He caught my mother and her together in a, you know, situation."

I was stunned, but I hardly imagined they were doing the same thing as Judy and Roberta in the toilets at Ravella High when the teacher on duty went ballistic.

"Then Alice *really* hit the grog. Your ma owes me big time."

"What were they specifically doing when he found them?"

"Puh-lease. Do you *mind*? *They have a special relationship*," she screamed. "Or they *did*. Alice doesn't know her anymore."

The sickly smell of bluebells blasted from Win's mouth. Tears brimmed on her lower lid. Her mouth went blue. I thought she was about to blubber all over the place.

"I was asking the question for purely scientific reasons," I said, trying to make her chill out a little.

The ammonia stench of the sheets was making me feel faint. And I felt as I had when I first discovered Father Christmas was a porkie. My imagination went into overdrive. Was Alice my natural mother? Had she and Namilly hatched up some mad plot to bring up their daughters in tandem?

It was possible. Win was older than I. If that were true, then who was my father? My skin was darker than Win's. Was it Orazio, the gardener at the house on Ti Point? Or Silvio Bjorkman, the Italo-Swede? Was I Italian? Had Namilly told me I was a Caldoche to throw me off the scent? Perhaps I was Jason Bjorkman's sister. (Thank heavens it was

Angela experimenting with *Merde! The French Your Teachers Never Taught You* instead of me.) Win was beginning to sway. Or was I beginning to sway?

She let go of the empty Polka Dot bottle. It dropped to the floor. She bunched her fingers into a fist, and screwed her hand into the corner of her eye. She was about to drop the blowtorch.

I turned to run.

She jerked the blowtorch up. "Don't even think about it."

"Where'd you get it?" I pointed my finger at the nozzle.

"It's Hank's. He's got a new job with Elizabeth's father."

I saw Stubbs' Bodyworks inscribed on the side. So it did belong to the bogan who'd attacked me in the bushes, the one who'd wondered if I had AIDS. He had said we shared a friend. But I never thought it'd be Win. What was she, always so neat and in control, doing with plebs like that?

"Do you realise he's the lowlife who attacked me in the bushes?" I cried.

She wasn't interested. "Get moving," she said. "You've got work to do. Load the machine. Mash and spoon the crud into her stupid face."

Was Hank outside, waiting to join our tea party? And was he the one with the snake tattoo?

Chapter 28

My jailer leaned against the door of the sunroom, watching as I tied a worn tea towel around Alice's neck. From time to time, her eyes flicked away from mine.

Was she worried she'd said too much about Namilly and Alice? And what had she really meant? I could hear the main bearing of the washing machine groaning from the weight of the clothes.

I pushed the spoon of yellow pap at Alice. She opened wide like a crinkled baby. She seemed to have all her teeth. She chewed and swallowed. Swallowed, then chewed. We were progressing well.

She suddenly gripped the metal in her mouth, shook her head from side to side. Her face trembled. I pushed and pulled but her mouth was like concrete.

Her jaw went slack, and the spoon flew across the room. Alice wept. I ran to fetch it.

"It's all you're getting, Mum." The tense, blurred look was back on Win's face.

Alice coughed. She spat. She dribbled. She pushed food out with her tongue. We continued to plough our way through the meagre meal. Slurping, mumbling noises as she ate. *Yum, yum, yum.* Harsh, excited breathing.

Alice eventually became bored with eating. "Body butter," she spluttered. Was that her signal that she'd had enough?

"What's she mean?"

Win shrugged.

"Wheeee, here comes the plane. Open wide." That aeroplane trick used to work with me, I figured.

Alice turned her head away.

She looked back at me with apprehension. Was she freaking out at the sight of an unfamiliar carer?

I was still bothered by Win saying Kingsley Winstone had caught Namilly and Alice together in a 'situation'. I'd never thought of Namilly having feelings for another person. I always imagined she'd go to her grave wondering. It was a shock to find she was human like everybody else. I had a thought: maybe she'd discussed my origins with Win's mother? On the other hand, it'd be a waste of time questioning Alice.

Without warning, Alice swatted the cracked bowl, sending it flying. Tumbling and wheeling, ochre-coloured food cascaded onto my joggers. I could feel the mush seeping through a gap in the canvas, targeting my toes and settling in amongst them.

"Go back to China, dear," Alice whispered. There was fear in her eyes. "Is it ever going to end?" she asked.

A fart filled the room and I briefly wondered if she'd done more than put in. I prayed Win hadn't heard. She'd go ape, big time, I told myself, squelching my way back into the kitchen.

My eyes latched onto two empty cans sitting on the floor near the back door. A Mayfair ham and a tin of pickled pork. *Hang on, weren't these Namilly's cans, the ones from home?* A posse of cockroaches rap danced in and out, inspecting, supping.

Everything was starting to fall into place: Namilly's disappearances, the pee smell, the antiseptic whiff. She'd been in this house, helping. Win'd never said, and I'd never guessed.

Now I knew about Alice, I wondered if Namilly would move in with her. Where would that leave me? As Win's de facto sister?

"Back to earth," Win's voice intruded. "Don't even *think* you've finished. There's more to do."

I stared at her moony face in the darkening room. "Such as?"

"Change her."

A panicky hiss in my throat.

Win jerked her head towards Alice. "She's messed."

No way.

"Shove it. I'm off! I, like, feel sorry for you and all that. But I've got exams. I don't *need* this. Anyway, you could've asked nicely, instead of playing funny twitters."

I didn't have time for this cry for help from Win. I had my future to worry about.

"Door's deadlocked." She bared her teeth.

"I'll phone the police."

"There's no phone. Remember?"

"Oh, I forgot. You're a troglodyte."

That mythical computer? That absent telephone? They had nothing to do with obscene phone calls to a fashion editor of a mythical magazine. The real problem was the bill at the end of the month.

I turned to leave.

"I'm so outta here." My dark eyes locked with her violet ones.

PUMP. PUMP. PHSST. PHSST.

I felt the heat of the flame from her blowtorch.

Chapter 29

I sat with my back to the wall in the dim room, desperate for a widdle. I willed myself not to widdle. No way did I want to end up like Alice. But I'd managed to change her without gagging. I deserved a gold star for that.

Win still refused to let me go to the toilet. "You'll scarper," she said. She was spot-on. I'd be out the window and off like a rabbit.

The night was black now. I could feel the cool easterly creeping through the cracks of the old house. Shadows of trees blended into one tree. No one spoke. Win gave me the odd glare, which was returned by me. So what were we waiting for? I felt deeply sorry for Win and her terrible situation. But what else did she want?

She kept sipping. Perfume bottles lay at her feet like fallen skittles. From time to time she sniffed and gouged her fist into the corner of her eyes, which were like roadmaps.

There was an edginess between us.

Alice was chirpy. She hummed 'Happy Birthday Sweet Sixteen'. She smiled her hummocky smile, clapped her hands, tilted her head and admired her reflection in the salty windowpane. Her image, highlighted by the indirect lighting of the chipped floor cones, was ghostly.

I glanced at my Swatch. Where was Namilly? She knew where I was. Why didn't she come? Did she want me to see what it was like living with Alice? Had she and Win hatched the plot together, used the bunch of flowers as a pretext? To see if Genna could cut the mustard?

Then I began to wonder if Stefan'd known about Namilly and Alice— whatever there was *to* know? Did Skye and his parents sit around in the evenings, rabbit on about it? Had Stefan written his letter out of pity? Had Jane donated her precious cowries for him to join together with sewing cotton to make me feel better about the whole rotten business? Were they meant to be *comfort* cowries?

But there'd been no unusual touching from Namilly. The opposite— not much touching at all. I'd always hung out to be touched.

A tap dripped in the distance. A cockroach scuttled under the skirting board. The wind picked up.

The television flashed colours. A tear of sweat dropped onto my hand. I began to recite verbs to fill in the time. Subjunctives. *Je fasse …* Voices in the street outside. The word *'révolution'*.

The veins in my hand were bulging like my bladder. I tried not to think about going to the toilet. The singing sound of a horseshoe skittering resounded through the house, followed by a suppressed grunt. I looked at Win but she seemed not to have noticed.

My heart began to do its own galloping thing. I said to myself, *Please don't let it be Hank.* I couldn't stand it if Win had me peeling vegetables for the bogan who'd trapped me in the bushes with his buddy. Forcing me with her blowtorch.

Or could I push the AIDS line again, cut myself with the knife? Bleed all over the food? I wondered.

Masculine legs materialised in the dimness of the hall. *No, not Hank? I couldn't bear it.* I lifted my eyes surreptitiously, scanned his arms. Hairy, but no tattoo.

Omigod, it was Marcel Manet. What was Marcel doing here? Last time we talked, he'd tried to make me believe Namilly was gulping down perfume, which had turned out to be Win. Had he come to bag Namilly again? Diss her with some other bright idea?

More importantly, how had he managed to get into Win's house?

PUMP. PUMP. PHSSSSSSSTTT.

Chapter 30

I soon worked out that Namilly had given Marcel a key, worked out that she actually *possessed* a key to the Winstone house.

We sat on the floor in silence, colour from the television flittering about the room. With her blowtorch, Win had made him back right off.

Beside me, Marcel examined the sleeve of his singed shirt, signature shades still glued to his forehead. He cursed softly, as if to point out that he'd almost suffered third degree burns to his awesome face.

I was sure Win had meant to miss him, assuming she was not past the point of doing anything expressly. National Service in the French army, he'd said, as he demanded her weapon. I wondered if he'd simply polished the wheels of the odd truck, cooked the occasional curry in the mess canteen, in light of his feeble attempt to disarm her.

I leaned back, pushed into his shoulder. He smelled of Gauloises Blondes and Kenzo aftershave.

Should I feel attracted to a man who could be my father? Was I destined to go through life wondering if all men were my dad, all women my birth mother, those of my own age siblings? And how was I meant to know if I was a chip off the old block if I didn't know who the old block was?

Marcel had been sprung by Win's postmodern burglar alarm: a wayward horseshoe. Then he'd peed her right off by shoving out his paw and pompously demanding she hand over her weapon. So she got busy with the pump, pump, pumping. Blue flames all over the place.

"I is trained by ze most efficient army in ze world. Be good girl."

With that, she had let him have it. And he collapsed to the floor like a soufflé cooked twice.

Win's ice-blonde strands stuck to her face, her eyes bulged belligerently, and I still couldn't work out why we were being held hostage. Alice snored lightly in her chair, her matted hair a halo of question marks.

"You sure you're not Win's father?" I whispered.

"*Non.*" Marcel rolled his eyes. "*Pourquoi tu penses ça?*"

Why did I think he was Win's father? I guess I was trying to make sense of everything. Anyway, it was a chance to practise for my oral, and his manner was overbearing enough for him to be related to my friend.

"*Cette garce, que veut-elle?*" he muttered.

He had me stumped. I had no idea what '*garce*' meant. I needed my copy of *Merde!*.

"Stop talking frog," Win suddenly screamed.

My kidneys were aching. My stomach was as taut as a tambourine. Now she had her second hostage, would Win allow me to go to the toilet? I raised my hand in the air. "Could I, like, be excused now? I am totally desperate to go to the luigi. You can shoot flames at *him* if I attempt to climb out the window."

Marcel swivelled his head, and glared in my direction.

"Okay, you can go, but be quick." Win hefted her blowtorch from one hand to the other. She looked wrung out, almost cactus. "Or I'll set your friend on fire, turn him into French fries. Don't even *think* about trying to scarper."

Doubled over with pain and trailing mash through the tear in my jogger, I rushed to the bathroom. On my way past the kitchen I caught a glimpse through the window. A person of familiar shape and size hovered outside. I gulped to a halt. Namilly was standing in the garden.

So, my mother *was* concerned about the goings-on in the Winstone house? She clutched a small glowing object, a torch of some sort. On closer inspection, I made out a mobile phone. But Namilly was terrified of mobiles. *Would she be prepared to risk cerebral carcinoma for me?*

She punched in numbers. Was she calling the police? If so, I'd be rescued. Free to join my V TRAMPS DREAM'N. Free to study. Surprised, I saw her hurl the phone into the bushes. Overarm with a spin-bowler's flick she dispatched the mini-Chernobyl to a safer distance. (I'd heard her hector Joe Stubbs, tell him Fat Betty would be consigned to a life cut short by radiation sickness, surgical intervention, chemo—half-headed in the end.) My heart became leaden. I seemed doomed to live in this house forever, cleaning up muck, caring for the Winstones. Soon I'd be laundering Marcel's ritzy shirts, and patching up the burn holes.

I slopped my way to the toilet, shoes slurping Alice's dinner. The sight of the toilet seat made me gag and there was no paper to clean it up, forcing me to squat. Dragging my jeans down, I perched over the splintered wood. With the denim at my ankles relief flooded through me. I gazed at the rippling cracks in the lino on the floor. If I could make Win see sense, my world would be back to normal.

In a nanosecond, a battalion of cockroaches scurried towards me at the speed of light. Having gorged on the residue of Namilly's cans, they'd come to search for their dessert.

My legs were in a material grip. I could do nothing but scream. Normally, I did not shriek easily. This time, I opened my mouth and let it all hang out. The fear and frustration streamed out of me as I hollered. I hooted till it hurt, till the roaches wheeled about and scuttled off in another direction.

I zipped up my jeans, and prepared to face my friend again.

"*Ça va?*" I could hear Marcel in the distance.

"*Ce n'est que les cafards.*" I yelled back, thinking if I kept up this French talk, my oral exam would be a walk in the park.

"Cut the frog speak." Win again.

I took my time, schlepped back past the kitchen.

Glancing through the window, I noticed Namilly was no longer there. Had she given up on the three of us, decided to let us rot together? I gloomily imagined her back in the comfort of our home, sitting by the fire, knitting bed socks from scraps of wool provided by Mrs B. Taking advantage of my absence by fossicking in my room, checking whether I'd received more letters containing leery descriptions. (The ground beneath the Norfolk Island pine at the bottom of the garden was overloaded already.)

Was she examining my box plants while I was held hostage by Win, checking the state of the soil, deciding if I'd neglected to water them? Placing a black cross on my report card?

I remembered Alice's flowers lying in a limp heap beside her padded chair in the sunroom. I should give them a drink and, perhaps in the process, help with her recuperation. That was, if sage and salvia and all those things really did make a difference.

I opened the grimy cupboard door labelled CONTAINERS, looking for a vase.

Win screamed in the background, "What're you doing? Get a move on or, I'll fry your friend."

I thought: *Chill out, Win. I'm dawdling in the interest of Korsakoff's research.* I could see scratched Tupperware, cracked glasses, mugs with chipped rims. A salad bowl. Nothing remotely resembling a vase. Then I struck gold beneath the draining board.

Beneath a CLEANERS sign, amidst bristly scrubbing brushes and bottles of weeping fluids, I discovered an elegant jar. The cream and brown label, torn and crinkled from having been washed, read *Fauchon, Produit de France.*

I scratched my head. What was a French jar doing here, all the way from Europe? Surely Alice hadn't really travelled overseas? Or had Win lied when she said those voyages were in her mother's mind?

The whirr of a helicopter sounded overhead.

Pigs in space?

My heart began to samba. At last, I would be rescued.

Chapter 31

The blade sound faded. Hope of rescue faded with it.

I filled the jar from the dripping tap, carried it back to the sunless sunroom and placed it on the ground beside Alice. I slid the slack stems into the water, and fluffed up the wilted blooms to give them shape. A pretty thing to look at while I remained in this surreal situation. Win's lips were like putty. Her hands were shaking. I could see the exhaustion was catching up with her. She'd become a carapace, like one of those empty limpets on the rocks at Ti Point, a long way from the vibrancy of the blue ringers Stefan and I hunted on a regular basis.

I subsided to the floor again. The warmth of Marcel's body beside me made my eyes grow heavy.

Alice, unaware I'd fixed her floral tribute, jerked awake. She sobbed quietly for a moment. Unexpectedly, her gaze became fixed on something through the window. Had her attention been caught by Bill Einstein grazing in the now darkened garden?

How often did Win take her mother to the toilet, I wondered idly, although the state of the seat said it all. Win Winstone was a fragile twig to lean upon.

"What is matter?" whispered Marcel.

I pointed towards Alice.

"She is who?"

"Win's mum."

"What is wrong wis 'er?"

"Korsakoff's whatsit. Korsakoff's Syn … *drome*, I think it is."

"Quiet!" barked Win.

Silence settled over the room, and I began to doze off. Marcel fidgeted beside me. Was he hanging out for one of those Gauloises Blondes poking from his pocket? A clock ticked somewhere in the house, an old-fashioned sound. How nice. Did Win wind it every eight days? Or was it a ten day clock? I mused.

Soon I realised the tick was from Marcel's watch. A whizz-bang monstrosity which allowed you to dive to the centre of the earth and back again without missing a beat.

"Namilly was outside," I muttered behind my hand, "I saw her through the window hurling a mobile phone into the bushes."

"*Merde*. It is mine. I give it to her."

"Radioactive waste," I whispered.

Marcel sat there sulking for a moment. "Zen she must 'ave went to Guesthouse. Skye is on duty tonight."

Slumped against her bentwood, Win seemed no longer bothered by our talking.

"How'd you know *Skye's* there tonight?" I hissed.

He smiled but did not answer.

I could hear the crunch of tyres on the road outside, low voices talking. More tyres crunching. More talking. Silence. Whoever it was had gone away, I told myself. My lids began to close.

"COME OUT WITH YOUR HANDS IN THE AIR." A megaphone filled the house.

I lurched awake.

Win sprang from her chair. Empty perfume bottles spun across the floor. Alice continued to gaze out the window. Marcel assumed a crouching position.

"Do you have any kerosene in there? Inflammable materials?" came the disembodied voice. The police seemed to be worried about Win sending us up in smoke. "Give us your phone number."

"There's no phone," she screamed.

"*Gaz lacrymogène*," Marcel said tensely. "Where is tear gas? Soon she ask for *hélicoptère*."

Tear gas? Of course, where was the tear gas? I hoped she wasn't about to ask for a helicopter as they did in the movies. I wanted out of there and back to my future perfect. To unload on Jules, as well, if he was in the chat room.

Win sprinted to the front of the house. A sound of shattering glass. PUMP. PUMP. PHSST. PHSST.

"*A million dollars and a rocket to Tullamarine.*"

Uh-oh, my friend had completely lost it. *A rocket*? She'd bought herself a ticket to the loony bin. I slumped back, thinking we'd be here for the rest of our lives.

Alice turned. I saw a grin on her face. She was radiant, her crinkly lines all but disappeared. Her eyes were alive. Did she know something I did not? This was the most fun she'd had in a long while.

I gave her a here-we-go-again look, glad somebody was having a good time.

"*Merde, merde, merde,*" Marcel muttered.

Precisely.

"Always told ya, son. Never trust a female. Nuthin' but trouble." Vince Becker's voice rang through the broken glass.

My heart twitched. Stefan was out there.

"Crime o' passion, son. All over you."

A murmur rippled through the crowd.

I was struck by a thought. *Did they think I was dead*? If so, Stefan would be chewing his fingernails away to nothing. Would he ask for my cowry anklet back? Or did he plan to place it atop the coffin as a token of his esteem, with a blue ringer in a jar nearby?

"Could 'ave, son. A real problem for those of the male persuasion. Nuthin' but trouble."

Vince Becker's words seemed to serve as a rallying cry. Marcel edged closer to the door leading to the entrance hall, a serious representative of the French military. Or was he simply eager to join the waiting crowd outside?

"Miss Winstone? My name is Dr Reginald. I'm staying in this peaceful village of yours. Perhaps you would like to talk to me, tell me your problems. I'm a good listener, it's my job actually." A pause. "Let me know what's bothering you. As I said, I'm a good listener. I have many patients with problems like yours. Feel free—"

PHUT. CRACKLE. SPIT. PHUT. Blue flames everywhere.

Win's flames were like dragon's breath. Nothing more from the shrink, Doctor Reginald. I ached to go to Win's side, would have but for Hank's blowtorch. I wanted to tell her everything'd be okay. She dragged herself back, eased herself onto her rickety chair.

"Hey, we're okay," I yelled. A flame hurtled from the other side of the room.

Unimpressed, Alice brooded. Sniffed. Mumbled.

Outside, all became quiet again. Had the onlookers tired of the ordeal?

Marcel reclined on the floor once more. His face was weary. His nostrils quivered. Was he imagining the bouquet of a ChâteauYquem 1908? Thinking of a dozen *huîtres de Bretagne*, *salade de tomates*, followed by a lightly cooked *sole meunière*? A *crème brulée,* perhaps? (I'd seen those luscious dishes in a Home Eco mag.) All topped off with a *café noir* and a fat cigar.

Or maybe Marcel was thinking of Skye Becker? My jealousy gene began to surge.

The shrink with the megaphone hadn't helped. And why did the fuzz not bring on the tear gas? I wondered. Were they all out that evening?

Time floated by like an invisible cloud. Alice continued to stare into the garden. Or was she entranced by her reflection? Perhaps she did this every evening? Would I be able to ask Win one day if her image was one of the things which turned Alice on?

Win was as uninterested in her mother as Alice was with her.

A slight movement came from Alice's chair, a lifting. She seemed to rise up; higher and higher; taller and taller, until she was as big as a mountain. Totally omigodish, upright and erect. Alice looked as if she were on stilts. I'd never seen her stand of her own accord, never imagined she could walk. Despite those little notes on the cupboards, despite Win telling me her pins were fine.

The room exploded into slo-mo action. Frame by frame. Alice lifted her vase-jar, hefted and swung. Brought it down on Win's head. And, like that, we were free.

Win's ice-blonde hair floated gracefully in a spreading puddle. Flowers were scattered about her. She was at peace.

Marcel lunged. He kicked the blowtorch aside, sent it swirling towards the flickering television. He seized Win's limp arms, wrenched them behind her back. Jerked his head in my direction and nodded towards Alice, indicating I should take charge of her. (Was he worried she'd go berserk, have designs on someone else's noggin?)

I threw my arms around Alice's thin body, and gave her a humungous hug. She remained passive, not returning the slightest pressure. Her rag doll hair flopped in my face, tickled until I could stand it no longer. I loosened my grip. The stale smell of her lingered in my nostrils, and I could tell she was going nowhere.

"*Une corde*," he screamed. "*J'ai besoin d'une corde*."

Where would I find a rope, apart from the one attached to Bill Einstein in the garden? I dashed to the kitchen. I scrabbled about in the cupboard among the triangular saucepans, knocking my knuckles on the nearby safety handle. I could only see scrunched-up supermarket bags. Not much, but they'd have to do.

I shook them out, smoothed them, and assessed them. Joined together, they could make a sturdy rope.

Marcel snatched the bags from me. He knotted them into a multi-coloured sissing cord, and trussed Win up until she lay there like a rustling mummy in a sea of salvia and wet plastic. I saw her give a teensy weensy smile, and I understood what this had been about: Winifred Winstone's war of independence.

Calm descended. White noise hissed on the television screen in the corner.

"We must take 'er—" Marcel began.

Sudden yelling. The glass at the back of the house blew in with a crash. Men in flak jackets streamed through shouting. An acrid smell filled the room.

My eyes were like a water spout. I fled to the front door, hauling Alice behind me—blind, sad and glad all at the same time. I gulped in the sea air, heaved it into my lungs, gasped in its freshness. The guys in blue would deal with Win.

A fine drizzle swirled and wafted. I opened my mouth, and drank it in. Just a short while ago, I'd been wondering if there was anything more to know about Alice. Well, I never imagined she'd knock out her daughter.

Chapter 32

Namilly hesitated, as though afraid to approach, as though I'd been transformed into an extraterrestrial being. I went to her, and put my arms around her. First time in a long time.

"*Nounou, Nounou,*" I blubbered into her neck. "It was like nothing else."

She didn't push me away. Her face seemed rounder, softer, and she smelled of sage. Gradually her features firmed, like sago pudding with a skin on top. Her raisin eyes became bright as polished steel.

I disengaged myself.

"You'll be alright, Genna. They need me now."

"Wow, I think I called you '*Nounou*'." I sniffed back the tears.

"No, you called me Ma. You know I prefer to be called Namilly."

Marcel loomed up beside us. "Madame, my mobile." He put out his hand.

"I disposed of it."

"I going to Grassberger's when you ask for help. Why you *do* zis wis my phone?" His blue eyes bulged alarmingly. He sucked on his cigarette as if to draw comfort from the heat of the glow.

"It was dangerous, and it didn't work."

"It not *work*?"

"I needed the password. You didn't give it to me. So I threw the phone away."

"But I say *révolution*. You *must* 'ave heard." His hair crackled as he ran his hand through it in frustration.

"I don't have time for riddles."

"When I say revolution I mean 1789, Frrrench revolution." His look challenged hers. But Namilly had already gone.

She bustled to the police car where a bedraggled Win was being stuffed into the back seat. She touched Win's cheek, and whispered some words. Reluctantly, she turned and went back to Alice. Wiped spittle from her mouth, and placed her arm around her shoulder in a protective movement.

The women manoeuvred themselves to the front steps of the clapboard house, sat down carefully, and gazed into the distance with resignation on their faces.

"When will it end? I want to go home," Alice moaned.

Stefan and Vince hovered at the entrance to Grassberger's Guesthouse. My mate was pale; pink patches shone through where the zinc cream had worn away. A Scotch mist swirled and hung as they hurried off. I gave Stefan a forlorn wave. He did not return it. I knew I never should've dissed his father about the cashier chicks.

No sign of Dr Reginald.

Jack Bradfield stood there still. "Onya, girl," he said. Then he, too, slouched off up the road. A Lacewing butterfly was pinned to the back of his tousled hair.

I ambled home. Beside me, Marcel puffed on a Gauloise.

"I told you to try chop-chop," I began, but my heart wasn't in it. "Y'know, Dr Reginald was wrong about Win."

Marcel simply looked thoughtful.

"Why didn't you stop her? All that PUMP, PUMP, PHSST, PHSST business."

"Is not toy to play wis flame. Poof!" He gestured with his hands.

"I wonder what's bugging her? She was always a cool chick."

"Perfume. Muzzer. Her problems is enough for anybody."

The police car edged alongside, siren silent, wheels scrunching. Win gazed blindly through the window. I ran to her. I scratched my fingers on the glass. I tapped, danced a little jig, anything to make her eyes light up. But the vehicle whipped my hand away as it sped off. Sirens behind blared in a cacophony, like a New Age funeral procession, only without the joy. Win was dead all right. And some of me died, too, as the cop car disappeared around the corner.

"You don't 'ave French plait tonight." Marcel touched my hair. "It remind me of my muzzer, Axelle. Your hairs are nice when you do like zat."

Shivers, I reminded him of his mother—no way could I tell him I'd never had that haircut.

"You read letter of me?"

"Yeah, I did. Some of it's under the tree with Serge Gainsbourg. The rest floated off, sank in Port Phillip Bay."

"What you sink of Sandrine?" He chewed his lip.

"A grouse story, very romantic."

"But she leave baby. She bad muzzer, you not think?"

"She had reason enough—the death of her husband, her love for Claude."

"He only Kanak miner." His shrug was dismissive.

"Rippling black muscles. Sounded pretty out there."

Marcel chuckled. He gave me two kisses in the French way, and then pulled the gate to behind me. He lifted his hand in a goodbye gesture.

"How did you know my email address?" I asked.

"Ooh, I guess."

"Yeah right, I s'pose you guess telephone numbers as well," I muttered, adding, "Then how'd you know the server?"

But he'd gone. His shoes flicked the dirt as he strode away.

Chapter 33

I scampered through the trees, past the canna patch where Win's cache of used perfume bottles lay hidden. Barrelled through the back door and slammed it shut behind me, gasping. Certain I'd called my mother '*Nounou*'. (Why had Namilly denied it?) And had she really been my nanny during those terrible Events?

The fire was cold. I scooped the ashes up in the dustpan, wrapped them in paper, and placed them near the door. I'd be in deep trouble if I scattered them on her garden, ruining her precious plants. Scent bottles in the soil? Fine. Letters and discs buried beneath a pine tree? Okay. Ashes on her garden? No way.

After lighting the water heater I had a soaking lukewarm shower, unable to stop thinking of my friend being held in custody by the Kingston cops. Were they making her sign forms about things she'd never said or done? Having arguments about what constituted 'flammable'?

I trailed to my bedroom. Dragging an old Mambo T-shirt over my head, I plumped up the quilt, hopped beneath it and tried to get some shuteye. I wriggled and tossed and twisted before finally giving up. I threw off the quilt, climbed out of bed, booted up and went online.

I typed in *babesinwoods.com*. No sign of Jules in the chat room. Skate and Billy Lid were there. We talked about my ordeal until my fingers became exhausted.

My hands are past it, I wrote. Logged off.

I went to the kitchen to crank out a glass of broccoli juice. Mooched to the hollow sofa to sit and sip and think about things.

What lay ahead for Win? I imagined she'd no longer be going up to the big smoke to stagger beneath the burden of HECS fees. (Not with a criminal conviction under her belt.) Lawyer? That was down the gurgler. Doctor? Forget it. So what was left for my immaculate friend? Tonight her life had collapsed like a castle of cards. She was left with a mother who was off the air, her days dominated by safety saucepans and deadlocked doors, with only Bill Einstein to talk to.

My eyes welled up. Soon I was weeping like a madwoman. I hollered and howled until my body ached. I hiccuped, wiped my nose on my T-shirt sleeve, and padded back to the kitchen. I delved into the corner cupboard for my emergency packet of Tim Tams.

I ripped open the cellophane and wolfed the lot down.

Would I grab a spade, unearth the other pages of Marcel's letter, reread his story of Sandrine Bas Salaire de Lyon's adventure with her Kanak lover? I decided I was too knackered.

The hollow sofa beckoned. Should I investigate its contents? Namilly'd never be any the wiser, I told myself. Anyway, I was sure she was looking after Alice and mightn't be back for days.

The lid was heavy. I heaved and shoved, attempted to hoist it up but it crashed down in a cloud of dust, narrowly missing my fingers. *An exam with my writing hand encased in plaster?* That'd be the pits.

Hoisting the lid open again, I spied hinged brackets in the far corner and realised that was how Namilly did it. I hoicked the brackets into place, bashed them rigid with my fist, and sat on my heels to survey my mother's stash.

There was the usual stuff: pickled pork, pickled cucumber, pickled something I couldn't make out—*ignames?*—the label in French, Mayfair ham, artichokes, gherkins, cornichons, corned beef, the edible root of the red beet, corn kernels, chick peas, aubergines, kidney beans, navy beans, butter beans, white beans, red beans, black beans, brown beans, citrus beans. And finally, cans and cans of normal baked beans. Namilly's methane factory was spread out before me.

I lifted up the tin faintly inscribed with the word *igname*. Did *igname* mean yam? Marcel had talked about yam festivals. But they'd be fresh from the earth, never in cans, I reasoned. The label was black around the edges, with botulism bumps on both ends of the metal. It was unlike Namilly to hang onto such a health hazard. Had she kept the tin of yams for sentimental purposes?

I placed the can back on the floor, careful not to cause it to explode and cover the walls with venomous vomit. I assessed her supplies. I now knew they were emergency victuals for Win and Alice. I'd never suspected, and felt cheated not to have known. (Not that I'd have eaten them, for they weren't raw.)

I was about to replace the cans when my eyes latched onto something unusual tucked away in a corner, difficult to see in the half-light.

I scurried to my room for a torch.

Shining the light deep into the back, I discovered other things. There was food Namilly had never pushed around on the floor. Exotic stuff I'd never heard of. *Oeufs de Saumon* in scarlet and gold. Iranian caviar in blue and gilt. *Foie Gras d'Oie Truffé* in oblong black with glittering trim. *Confiture d'Abricots* displayed in a tall glass vessel with a sign in cardinal red—Fauchon, 26 Place de la Madeleine, Paris. An elegant tin of *Thé au Caramel*. Jam labelled *Confiture aux Fruits Blonds*.

And, finally, a fancy ceramic jar of *Foie Gras Rougié, Depuis 1875, Sarlat en Périgord* (a white goose force fed and plump on the front, with yellow feet and wispy grey feathers standing in grass shaped like a court jester's hat).

I sat back, regarded her bounty with wonder. How had she come by all these things? As far as I knew she'd never been to Paris, had only mentioned living in New Caledonia. In any case, I was certain she would've refused to climb aboard a plane. I only knew of two people who'd visited the city of light. Marcel Manet, and Alice Winstone. (And I was unsure about Alice.)

Had Marcel given these luxury items to Namilly? They were strangers as far as I knew, despite Namilly having asked him to end the hostage situation. But the labels were worn. These goodies had been there for a long time.

I shone my torch into the corners again. Tucked away to the left was a red and gold box. Reaching inside, I lifted it out cautiously. I blew the dust off the label: *Pierre Koenig, Chocolatier, Metz*. It had never been opened. The chocolates would be stale by now.

I gave the box a shake.

A piece of netting, mildewed by time and the salt air, dislodged itself. I prodded the netting, tied with faded blue ribbon, with my finger. Adjusted my torch to find a *bonbonnière* of sugared almonds. Were these from Sandrine's wedding with Yves-Laurent Bas Salaire de Lyon? Had Namilly been a guest? Had she lived in Noumea before she knew me?

A wineglass, the stem in the shape of a prancing horse, lay near a bottle of eau de vie. *La Vieille Prune* was covered in dust and dead moths. An empty champagne bottle—*Clos des Goisses, Phillipponnat*, lay there too (Namilly hadn't buried that in the canna patch).

What did the presence of these items mean? That Alice Winstone had really been a fashion editor before she became a Korsakoff's victim? Were they gifts for Namilly, a reward for keeping an eye on Win? (It would explain the presence of the jar beneath Win's kitchen sink.)

I traced the shape of the bas-relief goose with my fingers, ran my forefinger across the beak. The back of my neck grew hot. Had I owned a toy like this ceramic goose?

I broke into globs of sweat. Was this connected to my sofa dreams? I threw the jar back in. A crack slashed along the neck of the goose, right where the grain would've been forced down its gullet by the Sarlat farmer. My stomach heaved. I ran to the bathroom and retched into the toilet.

Tim Tams swirled in the bowl, mixed with broccoli juice. Raw pumpkin, gulped while cutting up Alice's dinner, floated beside uncooked cabbage. Soon the whole icky evening was arrayed before me in the dunny.

Dawn light filtered through the squiggly glass of the bathroom window, a red tinge. Sailor's warning? My warning, too. I rushed back to the living room and hastily ranged the supplies in neat rows, terrified Namilly might catch me snooping. I let the lid of the hollow sofa down, and smoothed the upholstery with my fingers.

I needed shuteye. In a few hours, I'd be face to face with my V TRAMPS DREAM'N in Ravella Community Hall.

Chapter 34

A blowfly buzzing at the window. Birds scuttering on the roof of the hall. The shuffle of a piece of paper. Silence. A scribble. The sudden scratch of a pen. The rub of an eraser. A dropped ruler. Pencil stub rolling on the floor. Silence. The scrape of a chair. A seaplane droning overhead. The revving of a truck somewhere. Silence. A cough. A sigh.

Only a few minutes left, and I'd done all I could do in my written dissertation: *thèse, antithèse, synthèse*. My upper lip was tingling and swollen. A fever blister was in full eruption, consequence of my having bitten the inside of my lip in the ti-tree bushes. Or was it the tension?

"Put your pens down," boomed from the front.

I sat back, content with my performance. My V TRAMPS DREAM'N had served me well. I looked at the words, "*Il est sorti de la pièce.*" Fine, the verb to be was in its proper place. Then I noticed, "*Il est sorti tout son arsenal.*" Uh-oh, it should've been, "*Il a sorti tout son arsenal*", the verb to have on that occasion.

Those fickle V TRAMPS had let me down in the end.

My fingers itched to pick up the pen. I saw the supervisor's beady gaze as she strode down the aisle and decided not to risk it. I pushed back my chair, and reluctantly stood. Stretched and followed my fellow examinees. Now I was going to be even tenser for my oral, if that were possible. Stiff as a door for the next hour and fifteen minutes while I waited to go in.

I straightened my skirt, and lifted it from my sticky thighs. It felt weird to be out of jeans but I was determined not to look a klutz in front of my oral examiner, a Frenchman sent to Ravella to listen to me babble and stammer in his language.

I wandered to a shady bench under a peppercorn tree. I was second in, after Angela Rasmussen. She and Jason Bjorkman were holding hands, gazing into one another's eyes in an embarrassing fashion. For a brief moment, I envied Angela.

My copy of *Merde! The French Your Teachers Never Taught You* poked from the backpack at her feet. I strode across, peed off that Angela had been having fun while I was struggling to study, and search for my birth mother at the same time. Not to mention my ordeal with Win. Marcel, hanging around like a stalker, hadn't helped. Nor had the ceramic goose in the hollow sofa, surfacing unwanted memories.

"Gimme my *Merde!* back." I snatched it from her backpack.

"Cool it, Gen. Don't get your undies in a—" Angela's eyes bored in on my fever blister, growing more humungous by the minute. Her flyaway hair was a mad cap in the mugginess. She looked like a tube of kiddy toothpaste in her day-glo outfit.

"I don't s'pose you're even wearing any with which to get tangled," I spat.

I retreated to my bench, fighting my jealousy. I wouldn't have minded a one-man cheer squad to get *me* through the afternoon.

Hetty Geiger sat down heavily beside me. She extracted her pouch and her papers, and pushed her oversized, black-rimmed nerd glasses back onto her nose. She began to make a rollie, licked the paper, twisted the end, lit and leaned back.

"Chop-chop?" I pointed to her rollie.

"Mmmn, bit of the *you-know-what* as well to get me in the mood." She inhaled deeply, blew out blue smoke. "Like a toke?"

"Don't be a dork. I don't want to giggle in the examiner's face. Though you don't seem to be bothered by such a gross concept."

"It never affects me like that."

"Put the stuff away, man. You'll get sprung, have your whole year go down the toilet. My friend Win's done that very thing."

"Win always was a bit wacko."

"Whaddya mean?" I bristled.

"All that neatness, anal retentive."

"Well, *that* turned out to be a myth."

"So I heard."

"Put that away before you get sprung." I gave her a nudge.

"Nah, it's mulled up enough. Chopped mint, wood shavings, chop-chop." A droplet sat on the end of her nose.

"You'll be sick as a—"

My copy of *Merde!* dropped to the ground. A sketch of a naked woman with a cat on her lap lay in the dirt.

Hetty peered through her geek glasses. "Where'd you get that porno muck?"

"S'not porn, it's a grammar book."

"How come I never heard of it?" Hetty's Indian plaits were alive with curiosity.

"Word of mouth thing," I grunted as I picked it up.

The word 'mouth' reminded me that mine felt as big as a boxer's. The cold sore was taking over my face, and I understood how Stefan must feel with his lesions and zits. (He wasn't sitting this subject—too much punctuation.)

Beyond the peppercorn tree, Elizabeth Stubbs sauntered. Her basin hair fluttered in time with her legs as she smiled and moved her lips and had an imaginary natter in French.

Vonn Zammit, ground-staring brainiac, kept to herself. (There was an aura about Vonn. She came to class only occasionally, following every aspect of her Jewish faith as if it were carved in stone—which, of course, it was.)

We were an odd bunch sitting our final exam, females of every cloth, from Jewish to Caldoche and all sorts in between.

Hetty sat there puffing as if her life depended on it. Smoke swirled into the sky. I could smell the sweetness of the tobacco. Madame Mireille, all short skirt, bony knees and hennaed hair, flashed greasy smiles at a man in a silky suit. She waved her arms as if she were conducting an orchestra. A fat ring flashed on her pinky finger. I heard her call him Pascal.

Pascal turned and headed for the hall, the poky mayoral robing room to one side where we were about to have our verbal joust.

"Put it out," I hissed.

Hetty stuffed the roach end in her mouth, chewed furiously. Swallowed.

"Gawd, your guts," I glared.

She began to giggle and gulp. Her lips were scarlet and shiny.

"And *that's* a dead giveaway," I said. "Quit the giggling."

Hetty hiccuped. She folded her fingers. "*L'amour*," she said, as if she'd suddenly thought of something.

Why'd Hetty said that? Was she being turned on thinking about her oral exam? She had a freaky look in her eyes. She began to fiddle. She scrabbled in her bum bag, searching for food.

"Got the munchies?" I dug in my pocket, and handed her a banana passionfruit.

"What's this?" She eyed the fruit doubtfully.

"Fruit from our vine. Good for you, it's raw vegan."

"You'll get sick, you know, eating this stuff. Well, eating this stuff exclusively. Sure you're not anorexic?"

I'd never been asked that before. "Nah, not me." I flexed my skinny brown arms. "It's Namilly's greasy waffles I can't stand, the ones she cooks in her sunroom kitchen."

"What's wrong with 'em?"

"Makes me want to puke, the eggs and the fat and ..." I decided it was better to change the subject before Hetty had me marked as having some weirdo psycho disease regarding food. "Jack Bradfield been back, in your bedroom I mean?"

"Sure, the other night?"

"You're making it up."

"Nah, I've seen him and he's, you know, he hasn't been done."

"Hasn't been done? Whaddya mean?"

Hetty rolled her eyes.

I never knew what made Hetty tick, even though we'd been friends since primary school. She looked boringly butch but she might've been the most experienced one-hundred-percent person in the whole world. Or a non-event like me.

"I wouldn't know. I've only seen one guy's, in the scrub." I was boasting, I'd hardly seen anything at all that afternoon in the ti-tree bushes. I'd been so terrified that everything became a blur whenever I thought about it.

Hetty's eyes widened. "*Whose?*" burst from her mouth.

"Don't know his name."

"*What!*" Her breath was icky.

"I only know the name of his friend."

I saw the horrified look on her face. Should I confide in her about the bogans in the bushes? I wondered. It still sat there like a lump. I knew I'd feel better if I got it off my chest.

"Genna, you're next." Madame Mireille's arm made herding movements.

Angela walked, blinking, into the daylight. She embraced Jason with a satisfied smile.

"Let's go, babe." He folded her maxi jacket over his arm, and hefted her backpack. They walked off holding hands, swinging them happily and heading for the bus stop.

It was my turn to face the examiner.

"*Bon courage.*" Elizabeth Stubbs was wishing me luck. She sounded sarcastic. Her eyes gleamed as they fixed on my fever blister.

Descendre, Retourner, Entrer. I breathed the words. Go in. Go in. Go in. Forget about Hetty, Angela and Fat Betty.

Concentrate on those V TRAMPS DREAM'N.

Chapter 35

Goose bumps flittered along my skin as I stood before my examiner in his shiny grey suit. He made no attempt to introduce himself. Pascal looked as if he were dressed for a wedding.

I rubbed my arms with my hands.

"*Vous êtes frileuse, mademoiselle?*" he asked in a precise voice.

"*Frileuse?*" I froze. I'd never *heard* that word before. Great start to my final trial. Twenty-five percent of the first sentence my examiner uttered might've been in Russian for all I knew.

"Cold?" he offered in English. His lips went small.

"A cold sore? Yes, I think it is."

I touched my mouth. It was as big as my hand. Oh shivers, I should be talking French instead of blabbing on about my deformities in English.

He pushed the sketch before me.

I picked the paper up with trembling fingers. Where the hell were my V TRAMPS DREAM'N when I needed them? I'd spent so long learning them. Now they were leaving me when I needed them most. The black and white image seemed hazy.

"*C'est une fille,*" I said.

No, no, no. I'd called the girl in the picture a tart. I might as well've called her a full-blown skank and been done with it.

I corrected myself. "*Une jeune fille,*" I quavered.

I described the sketch haltingly. Then I recited a bit of Baudelaire without making too many errors, only pausing once.

He poked some Zola under my nose. I read aloud from *L'Assommoir*. (A sick choice, reminding me of Win's problems—reading about a grog-shop was *all* I needed.) I didn't understand the whole text, but I got the gist.

I did my own assessment of the man on the other side of the desk. Pascal seemed awesomely French—not a Caldoche, not a *poken* Australian, but a dinky-di, true blue Frenchman, a *z'oreille,* fresh from France. He had tight vowels and a taut body. He looked totally anal, quite different from Marcel Manet with his boat shoes, hip shades, and lazy island accent.

The conversation sailed along smoothly. I kept remembering my V TRAMPS, making sure I used the verb 'to be' whenever they were around. I gave the year we were in as 1802. The sunny weather was snowing. But, apart from a few hiccups, everything was going swimmingly.

I was fluffing on about Charles Bovary, husband of Emma, whose wife consumed arsenic to escape looking at his boring dial, when I made a boo-boo. A MASSIVE, HUMUNGOUS, GINORMOUS boo-boo.

"*Il a baisé sa femme,*" I said, straight-faced.

Pascal seemed startled, almost disapproving. Then he laughed and laughed until I thought he'd disintegrate. Teardrops sparkled in his eyes. His skin assumed a cherry glow. What had I said? What was so *hysterical* to make this odd creature crack up?

"'E ferked 'is wife?" he burst out in English.

Omigod, I'd chosen the wrong verb for to kiss. The one I'd chosen was the verb I'd heard Angela reciting in the blue bathing box. Oh, what a *dork* I was!

I fled from the wood-lined windowless examination room and burst into the sunlight, choking back the waterworks. My face felt like one mega fever blister.

Hetty Geiger, hearing Pascal's laughter, must've thought the exam was fun. She pushed past, eager for her turn. Her clothes reeked of chop-chop and charred wood and a touch of mint.

Fat Betty looked smug.

Vonn Zammit floated above the scene like a luminous cloud. (A brainiac, she'd never have uttered a doozie like that.)

I'd stuffed up in large lumps. My V TRAMPS? They were definitely DREAM'N in my oral exam. I was beginning to unravel like one of Namilly's handmade wool confections.

Chapter 36

I lay in bed for two days, plagued by sofa dreams. I writhed and sweated. The white goose pressed against me in the darkness, crying, " *'E ferkea 'is wife*." The ceramic goose cackled. It rubbed its beak against my face. It whispered, "Your name is Geneviève". "I'll be good, *Nounou*. I'll be good. I won't say it again." I heaved against the overhead lid, feebly tried to push my way out of the wooden prison.

On the third day, I went to the kitchen to crank out a carrot juice. Through the window, I saw Stefan standing at the gate. A white towel protected his neck. His face was a mass of zinc cream. His shorts were white. His Boomdogger T-shirt was white. He resembled a snowman.

My body ached. My cold sore had turned into a scab. I couldn't let my mate see I had problems with *my* skin.

On the fourth day, the smell of grease from the sunroom kitchen pulled me upright. Our place smelled like Burger King. Namilly was home. Her waffles were sizzling. I staggered to the door of her sunroom kitchen.

"So you're back?" I clutched my nose.

She did not reply. Her hair was limp. I tried again. "How's Winnie?"

"They've reduced it to a public mischief charge. She told the police she was planning to paint the house. They didn't believe her." Namilly's smile was wan.

"Excellent. That mean she's off free?" I was rapt.

"Not really. Pills, and condemned for the term of her natural life with Alice. The house does need painting, but I'm sure it was the last thing on Win's mind."

"Does she have to do an anger management course?"

"What's that?" Namilly absentmindedly turned her waffle iron over, and held it above the heat. Butter dripped onto her dress.

"Anger management, they rabbit about it on the telly and online."

"You do come out with some strange things. Of course not."

"Only the pills?" I said.

"Only the pills."

"That so sucks. Is Alice—" I saw the stop signs in her eyes.

I healed my wounds without help from anyone. No trauma counselling. I worked my way out of it solo.

Hetty rang. She asked me to go speed dating. I hit the beach instead.

Avoiding the rocks, the house on Ti Point and The Cauldron, I chucked a left at the bathing boxes. Peeling off my trackie daks, I flopped onto my ratty towel. I did what Stefan was never able to do: I sunbaked.

I bombed into one of those icky sofa dreams again. Grit was being stuffed into my mouth by the white goose. I felt myself scream.

I lurched up to find shrieking kids on holidays flicking sand at me with their thongs—a feral brat attack. Jason and Angela giggled nearby and I decided to get out of there. I hauled myself up, bundled my trackie daks under my arm and trudged up the burning path.

I moseyed through our garden, past the grevillea cubby, towards the canna patch. I could hear disjointed conversation, the odd unconnected word.

The fat on her flag arms flapped as Namilly dug in compost. She wore a shapeless straw hat secured by elastic and her chin was a waterfall of chins. But the thing that blew me away was the sight of Alice standing beside her. (Was salvia holding her upright?)

Alice was loony-lucid that day. I could hear her waffling on about China, confabulating. Her matted grey springs of hair squirted from the sides of a khaki pith helmet.

Namilly kissed her prune face. The signet ring flashed.

It was time to get back to the real world, go online with my cyberspace chums, time to search out our roots. Jules and I were meeting regularly. We were almost a cyberspace couple. And I had not told Stefan.

Marcel was waiting, seated on the front step. He punched numbers into his new mobile, punched numbers into his calculator, punched numbers into his watch. He pushed the packet of Gauloises Blondes down into his pocket as I approached.

There was not a crease in his Blanc Bleu ensemble. His boat shoes were impeccable. Even the slick of perspiration on his upper lip had a designer look.

I felt a grot in comparison. My trackies were gungy, my cossie was scungy, my tattered towel was cruddy. And the speccy man was perfect.

He pushed himself up, and gave me three kisses in the French way—an extra one for luck.

I shook out my towel, and plonked myself down beside him. I was still unable to work out why he was in Ravella but, nevertheless, I was beginning to feel more relaxed in his company.

"I is off tomorrow." He was straight to the point.

"Will you be back for Christmas?" I hoped he'd say yes.

"I no sink so."

"When will I see you again?" I felt a twinge as I spoke.

"Per'aps not ever. It depend."

"Depends on what?"

"'Ow sings work out." Marcel was playing his cards close to his chest.

I had a thought: "Did you ever give things to Namilly from Fauchon, you know, as a gift?" I was still puzzled by those delicacies I'd discovered in the hollow sofa.

He raised an eyebrow. "You say funny sings." He shook his head. His shades stayed stuck.

"No *Oeufs de Saumon*? No *Foie Gras d'Oie Truffé*? No *Confiture aux Fruits*? No *Foie Gras Rougié* in a sexy white ceramic jar with a goose in bas relief?"

"*Merde,* Geneviève. *Non, non, et non.*" He frowned.

"Don't call me Geneviève. I feel uncomfortable, it sort of bothers me, I get these goose dreams—"

"I sink you must seek counsel person to talk about your problem. I 'ave never met Madame Evian before I come to zis place."

"You stuffed up the brand of mineral water."

He smiled. A black cockroach with a white stripe scuttled beneath the house.

"Uh-oh, I left that bomb in the bushes."

"Bomb?"

"On the day of the bogans." I still felt edgy mentioning it. I willed myself not to go pink. "Well, have a good one, wherever you're going." I tried to sound cheerful.

"*Merci*. And what will you do on big night before?"

"Oh, the Beckers have a Christmas Eve bash. Jane gets pissed. Vince has it off with the cashier chick, and we all have a fabbo time."

My voice quavered a bit. Would it be the same this year? Or would it be different, with all of us moving on, tackling our affy year and those terrible HECS fees?

I discerned amazement on his face as he tried to imagine a Christmas Eve Becker bash. "I 'ave this for you." He delved into his pocket, and pulled out an elegant velvet box.

A small ring sat inside, too tiny for my fingers. Was this one of those Stefan Becker gifts? A body-offering that fitted nowhere?

"Great box. I *love* the box," I gushed. "Best box I've seen."

"For zere." He pointed to my toes.

I tried to squirrel my foot deep into the soil to hide the scar where Namilly had attempted to cut off my foot, expressly to ruin my love life.

"Try it," he said.

Reluctantly I brushed off the dirt, and jammed on the toe ring.

"You are what age?"

Why did he want to know that? "Eighteen, in a few months." Should I have racked up my age, said I was nineteen? I wondered.

"You seem more younger."

"I'm small, but I'm quite mature you know."

"And *wonderful* French plait." He put his arm around me, yanked my hair.

I felt a sharp pain, as if he'd pulled out a handful. Why was Marcel being so up close and personal?

"Ouch, an exponent of rough love?"

He released me. "You like?" He pointed to the ring.

I examined his present, a little passé, a bit last year's. "Cool," I said, "*très, très* cool." (Well, better than the faux bijoux I purchased in Kingston.)

He laughed, hauled himself off the step and strolled to the cyclone gate, past the flies squabbling over the spoils on the other side of the fence.

"*Joyeux Noël*," he called, before disappearing.

A smell of Gauloises Blondes wafted above the miasma. A purple sheen.

"Cool, or daggy?" I gazed at his gleaming gift. "Oh well, pressie from an older man."

But why? He was way too ancient to be interested in me.

Chapter 37

The blinds were drawn on Ti Point. Marcel Manet had gone. Win remained ensconced in the Winstone clapboard. His departure created a void in me.

Alice began to come regularly to our place, gardening with Namilly. No one in Ravella said a thing. The world didn't come to an end. It kept rocking along, with a few exceptions.

I hadn't spoken to Win since the night of the hostage situation. I decided I couldn't face her. Stefan said she'd changed. "Skye says she's a zombie."

"Has she heard from Marcel, Skye I mean?" I was anxious to know.

He looked at me strangely. "Why would she, mate?" He had no idea his sister had been seeing the New Caledonian.

Namilly continued to dig in her garden with a vengeance. She was up to her old tricks with the woodpile.

Eight days before Christmas, a letter arrived from the VCAA. I'd fallen over the line, passed my exams. I ran to tell her the good news. I could embark on the next stage of my life—maybe not in Victoria, but some place in Australia. My perfect tense had been less than perfect, but, all things considered, my V TRAMPS DREAM'N had served me well.

I was about to show her my marks when I caught her pulling a log from the bottom of the pile. The heap of wood cascaded into a mess of clutter, the classic oranges in the supermarket trick.

"You did that on purpose," I yelled, my ENTER score forgotten.

"Really? And what if I did," she smirked. "Fix it, Genna. You know I have a bad heart, and I'm not much good to you dead." Namilly still smelled of pee and antiseptic—even more and on a daily basis. But now I knew the reason.

Chapter 38

Panic-purchased items sat at my feet. I'd trawled my way through the Balmoral Shopping Centre in Kingston, on a mission to find a satin slip dress for the Christmas Eve Becker bash. All size 8s were for mountain ranges. Waistlines plummeted to my hips. Satin busts slid to my waist. Spaghetti straps flopped all over the place and, in the skinny stick-on mirror of the shop, I'd looked like a kid playing dress-ups in her mother's duds.

I knew I'd be forced to make do by wearing my tightest pair of jeans with a nearly-new off-the-shoulder black top—cheap as chips, on sale at K-Mart. I pushed the bag of candles away from my feet, skewed my head around. There were three of us on board. I'd positioned myself halfway up the aisle, against the window, so I could admire the view from Olivers Hill over Port Phillip Bay.

Skye Becker, all smooth-tanned and straw-haired, was devouring Sean O'Shane, surfie-toned, on the back seat as we ground our way up the hill. By the look of them, they would soon be having it off on the banquette.

I could see the driver staring in the mirror. I swivelled my head again. Skye extracted a voluminous garment from her bag, a sarong covered in magenta plums. She and Sean disappeared beneath it. Soon there was one large, squirming lump.

The driver licked his lips. His eyes were huge. I gazed out the window. *How embarrassing!* Were Skye and Sean doing it right there in front of everyone? Well, in front of me. And in front of the bus driver. Totally gross.

Attempting to concentrate on the scenery, I was unable to avoid seeing their reflection in the glass. There was mega activity, and no way to get away from this porn-in-your-face situation.

The silk slipped. A hand grabbed for it. Uh-oh, Sean O'Shane was mooning in the sunshine. (If Namilly'd been here, she would've buried him, Skye too, beneath the Norfolk Island pine tree.)

The driver's eyes were as big as soup bowls. The bus careened, swerved towards the cliff, threatening to hurl us into the sea. Cars tooted. Horns blew. He fought to regain control of the wheel.

A boat below hauled a water skier, a vast wake streaming behind. The skier would sure get a shock if hanky-panky skanky Skye plunged into the water beside him, I told myself.

The bus resumed its course. Sean and Skye sat up. They wound the plum silk about themselves and shrieked with laughter. Had they really gone one hundred percent right there on the seat? Or were they taking the micky out of me? Out of the driver, too? Would they be warned off public transport? Or welcomed back as in-road entertainment?

My heart calmed as the vista of the Bay spread out before me, sheeny and azure. A dolphin arced in the distance. Would Win have tried to do herself in on a day like this? No, I decided, it was too uplifting.

I should never have bought candles as gifts, I reasoned. What damage they could do to this wondrous scene. (Think of the problems the humble candle had presented to the Sistine Chapel.) But they'd been cheap, and cost was the bottom line until I received my pay for stacking shelves. I had a butterfly on a stick for Namilly, non-threatening in the global sense. The butterfly was handmade and had never clapped its wings to create a tidal wave in Mexico. It'd be fab for jabbing in the ground among the flowers when the pickings were slim. I hoped Alice wouldn't try to eat it. Or weep because it had no perfume.

I gripped my packages, and grasped the tubular back of the seat to steady myself as the bus pulled in at the stop beside The Store. I was the only passenger to alight. I could hear raised voices behind me. The bus sat there throbbing, and then took off in a cloud of dust.

No Sean appeared. No Skye. Had the driver made a citizen's arrest?

Thinking about this, my grip on the butterfly loosened. The wind snatched the stick from my hand. It wheeled across the road into the ti-tree scrub.

Uh-oh, I'd have to go in there to fetch it.

Chapter 39

I grasped my nose as I did when jumping from the high dive at Ravella Memorial Pool, terrified I'd bump into Hank or his mate in the ti-tree bushes. My heart was skittering as I chased my exotic purchase.

I scurried through the scrub, pounced and grabbed. Tempted to turn back, I decided to keep going—*it'd be okay if I hurried.*

The sun crashed down as I ran and I soon worked up a sweat. The coloured candles bumped against my side, the butterfly fluttering above as if it had winged its way from the tropical rainforests of the north in search of a less oppressive heat. I was a tad more upbeat about being in the ti-tree scrub. Nothing could touch me now. I was too fleet of foot.

My joggers, with the torn canvas over the toes, were still stained from Alice's dinner—a terrible reminder of that night. But I'd be gone from this place in a few months and Namilly'd be free to look after Alice. Win'd be free, too. If I could just discover details about my birth mother, life would be perfect. I ached to know everything. Serial killer? Shoplifter? Skanky ho? Fine by me.

Next thing I knew I was on the ground.

I lay there, mouth crammed with sand-dirt. Damn. How could I have been so clumpy? If not for Skye and Sean's grunge carryings-on I would've taken the main road, and walked in safety.

I lifted my head. The vibrant blue gift lay on the ground beside me. Its wire was bent, trapped in some sort of net. Were the bogans lurking in the bushes? I could feel my heart paddling.

I called out.

No reply. Seagulls screeched overhead.

I heard a cough. A male cough. A pair of white leather shoes covered in dust halted just inches from my nose.

"I'm terribly sorry, girl." Jack Bradfield's hair was awry. He wore a confused expression.

My heart was in freefall.

I lay there trembling, not daring to move, staring at him. How could Mrs B, with her whispery ways, live with such a person, someone who stalked the ladies of Ravella and did time for his lapses. No way would I enter the Zabaglione Woollen Shop again.

On the bus, I'd been wondering why he never climbed through my bedroom window. (I looked as enticing as Hetty Geiger while I slept, probably more so, and my clothing didn't stink of chop-chop.) Were the box plants on my windowsill the problem?

No matter. Jack was now stalking his prey in the daytime, with the aid of a net. I never should've chased that present I'd bought for Namilly.

I stared at his weathered, liver-spotted hand. I did my best to curl into a ball so he wouldn't have his way with me. Through the fog of terror, I saw his trousers were firmly zipped.

"Look what I've done, girl." His voice was sorrowful. "I've broken the wings of your Mountain Blue. Bit early for them though, usually take off in February or March. I can see it's not real now I'm up close. My eyesight's not what it was." He shuffled his feet in the soil. "Thought I'd had a stroke of luck, that the pupa might have come down on a load of bananas. That happened to me once. A green tree frog, poor little thing, tiny as my toenail. They looked after it at the zoo. I rang next week and they said it was fine. So, all's well that ends well, except for yer Mountain Blue. I'm sorry, girl. Ever been to the rainforests in Far North Queensland? New Guinea? New Caledonia? They're beautiful, wonderful. I go there, every few months. The Butterfly Sanctuary, help 'em out a lot."

Jack Bradfield folded himself into a seated position on the ground beside me. Terrified to move, I listened to him rabbit on about butterflies, the deep north. Rainforests.

"I attract 'em to the net with an old wing on my hat, bit like *you* attracted *me*. It flashes in the sun and down they come. On hot days, like today, they settle on the leaves hanging over the water." His mouth went small. "The Cairns Birdwing is a sight to behold. Big, green, bold black markings."

I relaxed a bit, eased my legs until I was sitting Indian-style.

Jack Bradfield was far away. His mind was somewhere near Kuranda in Queensland. I was tempted to flee while the going was good but, up close, he seemed like a harmless old man, engrossed in the world of Lepidoptera. As unlike Hank as possible.

"Egg's yellow or pale green on the underside of the leaves. They like young leaves, ya know." He nodded, caught my gaze.

I smiled, shrugged my shoulders.

"They don't like ferns." Was he in the mood to pounce? Was this butterfly stuff a ploy?

"Oh, what a shame," I said. "Why don't they like ferns?"

"Ferns have a nasty chemical, can interfere with development." He coughed. "Not many plants are suitable for babies, ya know. Blue Triangles on avocados, Eichorn Crow on frangipani, Birdwings. But the little fellers die. Very sad."

"I'm so sorry. Really, very sorry. Do you and Mrs B have any of your own, sons or daughters, I mean?" I'd never heard Namilly talk about any little Bs.

"No, girl, never been blessed." He was sorrowful. "But ya know what? The old Orchard Swallowtail's been tricked." A hint of a grin.

I felt it unfair that Jack Bradfield should be so triumphantly pleased about anybody being tricked. Maybe he *was* evil.

"On purpose you know, laying on parsley and the celery and camphor laurel." He paused, as if unsure about the camphor laurel.

"What happened?" I had to find out more of this mystery, this web of betrayal and deceit.

His face lit up. "The little fellers thrived. Can ya believe that?"

"Grouse." I breathed a sigh of relief, pleased for the Orchard Swallowtail. I was happy to find someone on this planet who could thrive on lies.

"Wonderful, isn't it?" he murmured. "And, ya know what?"

"What?" I found I really did want to know.

"They did even better on the parsley."

"Oh, I *am* rapt." I felt warm and fuzzy inside. Not only had they survived the deceit, they'd flourished.

I was glad for Jack Bradfield. He needed something like that to brighten up his life, being married to Mrs B with her copper bangles and her suspicious sniffing. I could understand why he climbed through bedroom windows to look. I would've done the same.

"Female instincts are not always correct ya know, girl." His rheumy eyes were stern.

I felt suitably chastised. Maybe Jack Bradfield *had* hit the nail on the head. I'd had no inkling that Alice was ill, that Namilly was caring for her, that they were close. Jack was right, female instincts were far from infallible.

A question was eating away at me. When did Jack Bradfield go to the rainforest areas? On community service? Would Win be forced to do the same?

"D'you do this whenever you get out?" I asked. "When you watch butterflies. Or trap ladies." I was getting confused. "I mean catch butterflies."

"Yes," he said, "when Mrs Bradfield lets me. She's a hard taskmistress, ya know. A hard woman."

"I'm sure she is," I agreed. (You'd have to be pretty tough flogging illegal tobacco without losing the *odd* night's sleep. And it must be hard to keep a serial voyeur in line, particularly one who chased butterflies when he wasn't chasing chicks like Hetty Geiger.)

"She's a feeding machine, ya know."

"Mrs B?" I was startled.

"In two weeks she can go to three thousand times her body weight. Amazing, isn't it?" He grunted and shook his head.

I realised Jack was talking about a caterpillar munching its way through dense leaves in the hope of becoming a magnificent creature who could clap its wings and cause an earthquake in China. (Alice Winstone would've been entranced by his tale.)

As I picked up my bag of candles he was still wobbling on about skin shedding and costume changes. It all sounded like Mardi Gras. I could hear him muttering that green and yellow stimulated feeding, that blue and red tended to stop them eating altogether. (Now *there* was a tip for supermodels—if they swathed themselves in red and blue, they'd never eat again.)

The sun was turning into a golden ball. I should get home, take a shower.

I tried to say goodbye.

He continued to sit among the ti-trees, whispering about toxic food plants, about how poison could pass through the gut unchanged, maybe even stored for possible self-defence.

I gave him a cheery, but ignored, wave.

He kept fluffing on about his butterflies.

My vibrant imitation remained enmeshed in the net beside him, and I groaned. Now I'd be forced to give Namilly one of those ozone-depleting candles. I'd be personally responsible for the demise of zillions and zillions of dreamy airborne beings.

Terrified of bumping into Hank, I ran home so hard my chest hurt.

Chapter 40

Sneakers slung across my shoulders, clutching my candles, I puffed to the front door. I could hear Namilly on the phone talking in French. "I'm sorry, but I will not allow it. No, she cannot meet you in Cairns after Christmas." A pause. "Why? Because she's beneath the age of consent." A sigh. "Well, you must have misunderstood." Another pause. "No, the fare is not the issue. I will not allow her to go." She tapped her fingers as she talked. "Are you trying to threaten me? Of *course* she is legally adopted." I'd never heard her say this before. "No, I was never her nanny, and it's none of your business."

Was Marcel on the other end of the line?

"No, her mother worked for *me*. She's no longer alive, I can assure you, and I don't care *what* you thought my daughter said." She drummed her fingers some more. "I will wish her *Joyeux Noël* on your behalf. *Au revoir*, Monsieur Manet."

I took a deep breath. My gut twisted into a knot. I'd just heard Namilly lie about my age. Why would she do that? And why should she care if I met Marcel in Cairns? I'd be gone soon, now that I'd completed Year 12.

Did my growing older bother Namilly? Was that the reason she kept shooing Stefan Becker away from our front gate? Could she see my mate and I were becoming closer?

I slammed the front door shut, whistled, behaved as if I'd rocked into the house without a care in the world. No way would I tell her about the fezz happening on the bus, or coming across Jack Bradfield in the ti-tree bushes.

I slid my feet into my sneakers and sauntered into the room, laces flapping and doing my best not to trip up from the tension.

"Any calls for me?"

Namilly shook her head.

"Only one, from Win," she said, as an afterthought. She looked away, and I knew she was lying.

"They have the phone on now?" I knew they did not.

She ignored my question.

"Well, I'm off to check my emails." I flip-flopped my way to my bedroom.

I booted up. Through the waviness of the screen I saw: *1 new message*. The email was from Jules.

We have such a lot in common, missing genetic links, all that. I think we should meet, discuss tactics. What about, say, Pedro's Coffee Shop in Kingston? Saturday? Will confirm time.

I stared at his message. My heart began to flutter. Was this an opportunity to find out more about my origins?

About to hit Reply, I paused. Two guys had suddenly appeared in my life since I started to investigate my past: Jules, and Marcel. And neither through official sources. I'd have to think carefully about his invitation. What if Jules was, indeed, an internet stalker?

My brain began to fizz. I'd thought the same way about Marcel. So far, there was no evidence Marcel was a stalker. Jules might well be a genuine, crater-face teen.

Then again, what if …

I moved the arrow to Off. The screen seethed with black lines.

The cursor froze.

Chapter 41

Four o'clock, his follow-up email had said. *I'll be carrying a red carnation.*

Whammo! The words '*red carnation*' ought to have warned me. Only a dorky middle-aged codger would've thought of that. Cross on the left ear lobe. Stud on the side of the nose. Strawberry mullet hairdo. Reflector shades. Flaunting a PalmPilot. Rapping Eminem. There were multi hip things he could've suggested. But there he was, holding his flower, froth on his moustache from the cappuccino.

Jules was a lulu. Same age as me? *Give us a break*. He was old enough to be my dad, older even than Marcel Manet. Grecian 2000 hair, dressed in a striped business shirt, clutching his floral contribution.

I didn't go into that coffee shop in Kingston. I stared through the window at my cyberspace chum, then caught the bus back to Ravella.

I thought about Jules—a dinky-di net stalker—as I battled with the water heater in the bathroom. The heater shook, rattled and rolled. Refused to turn on.

I had used nearly a whole packet of soggy matches, and was beginning to wonder if I'd be forced to endure a frigid shower. Either that, or suffer wog comments from Angela about 'some people' hiding their money under the soap.

The heater fired with a bang. I jumped back, grasping my eyebrow. Singed? *Although it could be kinda cool to have only one eyebrow at the Becker bash.* Soaping myself, I wondered if Jules had discovered my address. He seemed to be homing in. Marcel had discovered where I lived. Jules could do the same.

For the moment, I had more important things to think about. Like, what would I wear to the Becker bash?

I wrapped a towel around my body and padded to the bedroom. Clad in my leopard-print G-string, I opened the wardrobe door. I had few party clothes and not one satin slip dress. I eyed a maxi-skirt I'd worn to the school formal—the evening a disaster when Arch Biddle and his mates gatecrashed and the teachers chucked a berko—in the middle of the year. No, boring.

My eyes lit on a rather speccy confection, an off-the-shoulder frock I'd always liked. I could wear that again.

I lifted it out. The dress was retro, a little square dance number, cute and silky in faded rose—a for-the-boys thing. I saw the stain at the front, peered. Had I spilled a drink? Or was it something more sinister? Like leftover lust from last summer?

The mark was like a map of Tasmania. I shoved the dress back in. Nothing for it, I'd have to wear jeans.

I possessed five pairs of jeans in various stages of newness. I pulled out a dark stretch pair, hardly worn. The elastic in the fabric made them body hugging. I would look slick in those.

I hauled them in the direction of my hips. I tugged. I yanked. But they were mega tight. I eased them towards my tush. Had I become pudgy while studying?

I lay on the floor, eased them up further. A fingernail snapped as I hoisted them over my hipbones. But the zip remained wide apart. I fiddled with the pull, egged it on, clenched my fist in triumph as it closed. Yessss!

All I needed now was something to wear on top.

I attempted to push myself up. I tried to roll over, but my legs were stiff as a plaster cast. I was trapped on my back like a beetle. Rolling and edging my way towards the bed using my elbows, I grappled for something to hang on to. Heaved on the headboard. I got traction, and was able to manoeuvre myself upright.

I stood there panting. How would I ever move at the party? I wondered. These jeans were like a chastity belt.

Goose-stepping my way to the mirror, I turned sideways. It looked as though I was strung together in one of Namilly's torture chamber corsets. I had a killer figure.

Way to go, girl.

Rigid, I fossicked in my drawers. The pickings were slim in the top department. The best of a bad lot was a boat-necked piece in black jersey I'd forgotten about. Why had I never worn it?

I held the garment up. The sleeves were long. The neck was high. Basically, it was spazzo. About to toss it on the floor, I examined the clothing more closely. It was fixable if I used my imagination. I could deconstruct it bit by bit, see what happened.

I picked at the threads with my broken nail, sank my teeth into the seam. Clenched and plucked. One sleeve gone. Should I leave it? I pondered. One-armed clothing was trendy at the moment.

After some thought, I opted to rip out the other sleeve.

Repeating the manoeuvre. I attacked with my ragged nail again, followed up with my teeth. *Voilà*. The top was sleeveless. I was getting somewhere.

Dragging the top over my head, I gazed at my reflection and lowered the neckline to show off my new tan. Speculated. Could I do anything with the spare sleeves lying on my dressing table? I fossicked for a pocketknife in my bedside drawer, and ran the blade along the torn edge.

The fabric curled and frothed like the waves over Selwyn's Fault. I intended to plait my hair to one side, tuck the plait neatly into my neck and tie the teased fabric into a ragged bow. Would it look too Morticia Addams? (Then again, Morticia would never have been seen *dead* in denim jeans.)

I wove my hair until the muscles in my arm began to spasm. Tied the stressed jersey into a frilly confection on the ends, and applied a scarlet lipstick I'd bought in Kingston. Finally, I gave myself a quick squirt of last year's Miss Dior perfume (a Christmas present from Namilly).

My gaze glued onto my right eyebrow. Definitely singed. I pulled out a brown lipstick and joined up the dots. "After a few champagnes, nobody'd notice," I murmured.

I dragged a pair of black sandals, studded on the heels with glass diamonds, from my cupboard with my toes. Slid my feet into them. With Marcel's toe ring gleaming, they were ultra-chic.

Uh-oh, I'd forgotten Stefan's cowry anklet. Would he be hurt if I didn't wear it? I looked for his gift, but it was no longer in the bottom drawer. I scrabbled in my bedside table. Tossed out Post-its and peanut shells and pencil stubs. The cowries weren't there. Had Namilly taken them? She'd been acting kind of weird since that telephone call from Marcel, staying at home more, going less to Alice Winstone's.

My eyes swept the room.

In the lowering rays of the sun I saw Stefan's shell creation, lying on the windowsill between two of the terracotta pots. I decided Namilly must've been in my room, found the anklet, and left it there for a reason.

I picked it up. Cut leaves fell to the floor. Blast. I'd forgotten. *It was clipping day.* I flicked the pages of my diary to the twenty-fourth. Yes. I'd marked the date in pencil. Was this her way of paying out on me, using those shells in some sort of twisted statement?

I slung the cowries over my wrist, held my arm horizontal to prevent them from falling. I was goose-stepping my way out of the room when I remembered I'd hidden my present for Stefan, a purple candle with an orange wick, under the bed. However would I get down on my knees to reach it? I asked myself.

After thinking of various positions, I figured the best way was to do a one-handed reverse pushup.

I collapsed in a flurry of house dust. The shells flopped around my weight-bearing hand as I dragged out the bag marked *non-genetically-modified candles*. The bag was covered in garden soil. Namilly'd been having a great old dig around. She'd been seriously snooping this time.

Clutching Stefan's candle, I lay there for a moment, my mind whirling. What was Namilly's problem? Was it Marcel's call? Alice? Or something else?

A wedgie was killing me. I reached for the angle iron, and hauled myself towards the headboard. As I swung up, my black top sprang back over my shoulders like a slingshot. I chased my spangled sandals with my feet, and edged them on.

Breathless, I sallied forth.

"I'm off, Ma."

I marched through the living room, past the hollow sofa where Namilly perched with a thunderous look on her face.

"You coming?"

"Later." She scowled.

"Well, better turn up before they run out of grog, like always!"

I clicked my way past the flies feeding on Namilly's cans, lugged my top down as far as it would go, and headed for the Becker's.

Chapter 42

It was a stardust evening, a cream puff of an evening, filled with birds and bats and yummy winged creatures. The twilight was floating away, chased off by the darkness. Cinnamon specks of flock and strips of palest lavender dotted the density. The night was fragrant with the smell of cut grass.

The resonant hum of humans, rising and falling, wafted towards me. The odd shriek of laughter, as if someone had said something terribly funny, cut through. I felt floaty and excited. A new chick I'd met up with in the chat room, Elise, could be the answer to my search for birth mother information. I aimed to contact her later.

The cicada buzz of people burst in my face as I skirted the hedge and turned into the Becker's front drive. I was funky that night in my black jersey and straitjacket denim jeans.

A huddle of guests gathered beside the mossie zappers which cracked and spat as, one by one, the insects bit the dust.

As I passed through the front door I saw Stefan descending the stairs. He strolled past the faux chandelier where uncool decorations clung to flame-shaped light bulbs. Clad in PVC, he crackled as he walked. I gaped. It was as if a big white chrysalis had opened up, disgorging this night-time life form. Stefan was like a massive moth in black plastic. Hot.

I dragged my top down further. His skin, sans zinc cream, was clear that evening. I discerned only one knob beside his eyebrow, a tiny scar, a remnant of a lesion. Not one zit.

"*Joyeux Noël*," I breathed.

His eyes wandered across my clothing. "G'day, mate." He brushed the dust from my bedroom floor off my cheek, and glanced at the cowry anklet swaying on my wrist.

I thrust the purple candle at him. "Sorry, not wrapped," I giggled.

"Thanks, mate." Stefan stuffed the candle into his pocket. Only an orange wick could be seen.

"Hope no one sets you alight," I chortled.

"Hair's neat." He eyed my French plait, took my hand.

"Um, thanks. Where're we going?"

"Jane commands, there's stuff to do in the kitchen."

"How so boring." I made a face. "What, for example?"

"Daggy dips." He grimaced.

In the kitchen Jane Becker was filling trays with goodies: canapés, club sandwiches, nori rolls. The highlights in her hair were aflame. She gave me a nod and got on with it.

"Stefa-a-an, if you don't get those dips out the crisps'll go soggy." Her hips, in luminous white, waggled as she worked. "Have you seen Skye? Probably with Sean. She's like her father. Nobody ever helps me."

We grabbed a platter each and fled. I stopped, fizzled my finger into the pink goo and rolled the dip around on my tongue.

"What *is* this? S'great." I licked my lips.

"Taramasalinguis."

"You mean *taramasalata*." I couldn't seem to stop giggling. "What's yours?"

"Tsatsiki."

I pushed a finger into his dip. "Prefer mine," I said as I tasted, and then remembered my raw vegan diet. "Not yogurt, is it?" I began to panic at the thought of dairy food inside my body.

Stefan nodded.

"Shivers, that means milk." I saw the disapproval on his face. Was my veganism bothering him?

"What's wrong?"

"You double dipped."

"I did not. Hey, do the dips come from the Greek café on the highway? Or Kingston?"

"Acropolis on the highway."

"Namilly says they use dogs."

"Dogs in their dips?"

"Well, in those mince and vine-leaf thingies. You wouldn't want to eat Mrs B's Jack Russell for dinner, would you?"

"She's a retard."

"Who? Mrs B?"

"Nup, your mong of a ..." I knew he meant Namilly.

"Well, let's dole out those dicky dips," I said, subdued for a moment. Stefan had a point about Namilly, but she was my problem, not his.

The taramasalata tasted terrific. I planned to eat as I worked.

A scream from the other side of the room. Angela Rasmussen's gaze roamed down Stefan's plastic daks.

"Pleased to see me, Stef?" she cried.

Jason clutched her and they fell about laughing. I felt like hitting them over the head with my French book.

Fat Betty, chubby-cheeked and azure-eyed, smirked. Her basin-cut hair gleamed under the light of the fake chandelier. She fluttered her fingers over her pink satin slip dress. (The colour blended with her legs.) She began to fiddle with the garnets around her neck. In her drooby way, I could see Elizabeth was trying to flirt with Stefan. (Well, I didn't have her garnets, but I was wearing a gift from an older man.)

While admiring Marcel's toe ring, I felt the corn chips coursing down the tray and onto the floor. I tried to cover them with my sandal. They made a hyper-crunchy noise. I pushed my way to the other side of the room.

From where I stood, a gross birdcage effect decorated the burgundy wall-to-wall carpet. I hurried to the lawn outside before anyone dobbed me in. There, I scoured the inside of the empty bowl with my fingers. I buried the empty tray in the bushes, rather than face Jane in her kitchen.

I heard a voice. "Cod's roe in the taramasalata. That's what gives it that wonderful salty flavour."

Gulp. So *my* dip hadn't been raw vegan, either. *What should I do?* Ram my finger down my throat? Throw up in the bushes? Or rationalise it as brain food and forget about it? I tossed up the options. Exams were over. Brain food didn't count anymore. But if I didn't make up my mind soon, it'd be too late to do anything. That cod's roe would be trundling through my gut.

Hetty Geiger choofed on a rollie beneath a nearby acacia. I had no time to talk to her—no time to diss Elizabeth, or to discuss the perfect score of fifty points Hetty'd received for Australian History.

I headed for the sunken garden to operate on myself.

Chapter 43

The sunken garden was a 'remorse gift' from Vince to Jane, one of many 'remorse gifts' in the Becker household. They ranged from major items, such as the burgundy wall-to-wall carpet and the plastic chandelier, to minor things, like the el cheapo *'Tis Here* sign on the door of the loo. The sunken garden, in which I was about to make myself throw up, was the place I'd done my test-run kiss with Stefan—eyes closed, mouth tight shut, on my thirteenth birthday.

We'd never progressed to full-blown girlfriend and boyfriend. (It was all to do with those facial impediments. His skin problems had suppressed my primal urge right down to hypothetical.)

I nearly cannoned into him easing out of the kitchen door.

"What're you *doing*?" I hissed.

"Escaping," he grunted.

"Stef-a-a-arn," came the muted scream from the kitchen, "the cat's eaten the moussaka. I *told* you to put her in the laundry. *Stef-aaarn*, what are we going to do for the main course?" A pause. "I *know* you're out there, you'll pay for this." A hoarse pause. "Get your sister. I'm sure you know where *she's* hiding."

Stefan's body was rigid.

I crossed my legs to stop from giggling.

Jane's hectoring slowed, and gradually became silent. Stefan's breath expired like a balloon set free. His body turned limp.

"Fed up with the party?" I grinned.

"I'm no farmer."

"Farmer?"

"Lot feeding." He pulled me towards the sunken garden.

We tumbled down the steps and collapsed onto the lawn beside his mother's hydrangea bed.

"What happened here?" I ran my fingers down his face. The spot over the back door cast a glow across his cheek.

"Cortisone." His eyes slid away, as if he were ashamed.

"You planning to use cortisone all the time?"

"Can't, makes you blow up." His hand gripped mine as if it bothered him.

So we sat there, taking in the peace and quiet of the crater space. My legs were stretched rigid before me from the tightness of the denim. My jersey top gripped my arms like an angry blue ringer.

Stefan slowly withdrew his hand, and placed it around my shoulder. He began to rub gently. It felt good. A place I could relax in.

Next moment, everything was different. For the first time, ever, Stefan began to grope. He attempted the round-the-shoulder-and-down-the-front-of-the-top routine. I felt tingly all over.

He froze for a moment.

"S'okay," I murmured.

My heart did a jiggle. Stefan was on the road to becoming a craggy man. I squirmed around, lifted my face towards his amazing new one and ran my fingers through his hair.

The killer kiss came next. The melding of the tsatsiki and the tara-masalata. My mouth melted into his. I could feel my head being consumed. I was turning to jello. He was swallowing me up, right down to the tips of my toes. And there were no more lumps and bumps. We were one stunningly smooth super human being.

Emerging from his kiss, and able to think again. "Sorry—" I began.

"Shut up." His voice was hoarse.

"Okay, carry on Romeo."

My body was getting the most incredible massage. Well, the bits that weren't hemmed in.

I reached for the zipper of my jeans so that he could explore further. I tugged on the pull. The zipper was stuck. I tugged and tugged, but it was no use.

A sudden ripping noise. My jersey top slithered to my waist. Uh-oh. *How would I get home with my upper torso naked*? I pushed the problem to the back of my mind, pressed on across the PVC. Stefan began to groan. (I never knew guys groaned.) The groans developed an agonised edge.

"They're *killing* me," he moaned.

"What are?"

I would've sat up, but his body had joined ranks with my chastity jeans in pinning me down.

"Lover's ooh … ooh … *ouch*." He groaned and ground his teeth.

"What'll I *do*?" I hissed. Wedged beneath him, I was unable to move.

His moans subsided to a whimper. My French plait was now tangled in a hydrangea bush. With a pop my zipper burst and I was free, sticky in my deconstructed straitjacket.

Stefan continued to pin me down. "Uh-oh!" he said.

Should I make polite conversation? I wondered.

"I am so going to clean up." I tried to push him away. But I was like one of Jack Bradfield's butterflies on a board. And Stefan was even tenser than when his mother'd harassed him in the kitchen.

"You okay?" I disentangled my head, peered at him.

"Mmmmn," he murmured, face down in the darkness.

With a heave, I managed to roll him off me.

I turned on the garden tap and held my hands under the water. For the first time that evening I was glad I'd never bought a pink satin slip dress.

"You still on this earth?"

Stefan breathed heavily.

"What're you gonna do now?" I gathered my jeans together, hauled down what was left of my top, and covered my busted zip as best I could. "That kiss was great. It was, like, a *killer kiss*," I blurted.

Stefan didn't answer.

"But I think we, like, flunked the more advanced part."

"Oh, *shut it*!" floated from the flowerbed.

Stefan pushed himself up. His hair was awry. He began to tuck in his shirt. I saw a new eruption in his eyebrow hairs.

I climbed the steps of the sunken garden, hugging the remains of my top. Behind me, Stefan made trailing noises. His PVC was fluttering. We'd never got around to discussing that letter of his, and now I'd blown it. But, if it hadn't been for those jeans of mine, we might've gone all the way that night.

In the kitchen, Jane gave us a berko look. We had twigs in our hair. Our clothing was stained. Stefan, wearing more lipstick than I, was whey-faced. My gear was flopping all over the place. It probably looked as though he'd tried to rape me.

"You two could do with freshening up," she said.

She began to stir the spaghetti, replacement for the moussaka eaten by the cat. She muttered, "Another one gone, the whole frigging family."

I left to find the bathroom. As I let the swing door go, I saw her tip her champagne into the pasta.

"You stink of perfume!" she said to Stefan.

Chapter 44

I fled towards the staircase clutching my duds. Shedding leaves as I went. The guests, having socked down enough Christmas cheer for the night to have become a blur, ignored me. What would've happened if I really had been roughed up? Probably nothing. A scary thought.

Florence Stubbs noticed, though. Her hair was in a plastered-down bob, her eyes two disparaging slits. Florence was a racist. She bagged Silvio Bjorkman, the Italo-Swede father of Jason, big time. ("He's a WOG," I'd heard her say to her husband when Silvio left his glitzy, souped-up, second-hand Commodore to have the bingle beaten out of it at Stubbs' Bodyworks.) I was not born a Skip. Did she feel the same way about me?

As a teenager, Florence had strutted her stuff across the screen in *On The Beach*—the movie about the end of the world shot on the Mornington Peninsula. An extra, with no lines to learn, she remained a drama queen. That film was the only interesting thing to happen in her boring life.

No sign of Namilly. First time I could remember her missing the Christmas Eve bash at the Becker's. Just as well, I told myself. She'd be spewing at the state of my clothing. I assessed the situation. Should I hang around, aim to get home after she'd fallen asleep? *If* I was able to tidy myself up.

On the other side of the room Sean O'Shane flirted with Annie Bright. Her freckles folded away into her eyes as she laughed. And she was laughing a lot, flopping about like a landed fish at everything he said.

Skye was up for air and unconcerned. She floated around like a gracious hostess in her mauve mini-skirt. (Did the embarrassment and jealousy genes not exist in the Becker family?)

Should I ask Skye for a loan of a T-shirt? I wondered. As a laundry consultant she was bound to have tons of T-shirts. Recalling the incident on the bus, I decided I didn't dare. I headed for the bathroom.

"Bitch!" A hissy voice floated up the stairwell, directed at me. Elizabeth sounded stroppy.

In the bathroom, I examined my reflection in the mirror. A magpie's nest of twigs and leaves was buried inside my French plait. I began to pick the bits out, watched them drop to the floor as I pondered: How to reconstruct my top?

Leaves dealt with, the only solution that came to mind was to tie the scraggy ends into a bow. I yanked and twisted. The fabric across my arms became scarily thin. The gap at the front was my main problem. Should I take it off, wear the garment back to front? Could look sexy.

I positioned my fingers on the hem, began to lift my arms. A smoothly-tanned hand reached around my shoulder, and placed two safety pins—ends lacquered in blue—on the bench before me.

"You're indecent." Skye Becker, hair upright and blonde-tipped, gave me a cool smile, as cool as her mother's had been. (*Indecent*? A bit rich from a person comfortable with mooning in the sunshine.)

Returning her smile with an even frostier one, I kept reconstructing with as much dignity as I could muster. Skye's safety pin was a mega help. I was able to join the neckline together. If I pinned on a flower, it'd look moderately elegant. Top problem solved, I needed to work out what to do with my jeans. With my leopard-print G-string showing, I looked a total skank. I skewered in the second diaper pin, creating a bridge across the print. Which was kinda weird.

I hauled down my top, managing to cover the disaster zone with only a millimetre to spare. As long as I remembered not to raise my arms, I could survive until it was safe for me to leave the party. Had I gone from cool to tacky? Was I mint? Or simply interesting? I wondered.

I rearranged my plait, retied the ragged bow, and tucked the plait into the hollow of my neck. A stray gloss lippy lolled on the marble. I smeared the purple on, and surveyed the overall effect. Not va-va-voom. Just a tad less 'indecent'. I could see no pash rash on my face, no love bites on my neck from the snogging.

I bounded down the stairs to find Stefan.

He was nowhere to be found, not in the dining room, the study, nor the kitchen. Then I saw him ambling down the stairs, showered and changed. He wore clean jeans and a scarlet rugby jumper. He looked cool in his new gear, like Kurt Cobain. A total chick magnet.

I went gooey all over. I waved but he veered off, ignoring me as if I'd suddenly become the town tart.

I decided to pluck some petunias from the garden, fill my top to overflowing. With luck, the fabric would hold out until I left.

In no time, the petunias began to wilt. But the old men didn't seem to mind. Vince Becker, sandy hair spiky, hands smelling of dollar dosh, flung his arm around me as I passed. I wriggled away, only to be accosted by Joe Stubbs. I did a neat sidestep. A finger jabbed into my derriere. Tweaked. My breath sucked in. *Joe Stubbs. Had just. Pinched me*.

Stefan, watching from the other side of the room, frowned. I felt a squirt of pleasure.

Angela and Jason were playing cannibals on the couch, so into one another that it was embarrassing. Hetty Geiger, eyes huge behind her nerd glasses, leaned on the arm of the couch watching. Silvio Bjorkman played with the ends of her Indian plaits, burying his nose in them. It was a hippie scene, sort of like a flower power love-in daisy chain.

Gross. I turned away. Silvio was employed in one of those weirdo jobs where no one knew for certain what he actually did. Ravella people whispered that he worked for ASIO. If so, was he sniffing for chop-chop? Would the Zabaglione Woollen Shop be raided, Mrs B arrested?

I needed to leave. No way did I want to be interrogated for using an illegal substance, stuff up my affy year as Win had.

Fat Betty was homing in on Stefan. He glanced in my direction with a smirk. What'd *I* done?

Jane's bowl of spaghetti sat on a side table, ignored and cold. Strands dangled over the side, sticking to the ceramic in interesting squiggles.

"Off to replenish the grog, folks," Vince shouted.

The room exploded with laughter. (They knew where *he* was going.)

Jane, all cool eyes and confidence, put on a disc and began to jive to the music of *Hot August Night* with a man called Stan.

Outside, I sauntered past the cracking mossie zappers. Through the window I spied Elizabeth—potential dudette—drag Stefan—total Kurt Cobain—to the fake chandelier. Mistletoe dangled from a flame bulb.

He bent his head and kissed her.

Chapter 45

A flash of lightning on the other side of the Bay. A lurch in my stomach.

Everything was going wrong. My virtual boyfriend, Jules, had turned out to be a net stalker. My real-life boyfriend, Stefan, had kissed Fat Betty. Now all I needed was for Namilly to be awake and waiting and in questioning mode.

I closed the front door behind me, and crept past the oak armoire. Apart from Marcel's call, I had no idea why she should be so fizzed off with me. Unless she'd noticed I'd been poking around in the hollow sofa, seen some of her cans out of order. Or was it the clipping ritual, the plants I'd forgotten to help her with? (Those footprints on the floor had looked angry. Was she trying to tell me something?) And was the placement of Stefan's shell ankle bracelet among the cut leaves some sort of warning?

My wrist felt light. I glanced down. My arm was bare. Had I left Stefan's cowries in the Becker's sunken garden? No wonder he'd been so remote, I told myself. I seemed to be bugging everybody lately.

Sandals in my hand, I padded towards my bedroom.

"Do you have something to tell me, missy?"

I started. Namilly stood in the doorway. She looked mad. She looked mumsie. She had rainbow sponge rollers in her hair.

"*Wh-wh-what* do I have to tell you?"

I loathed those nerdy guessing games she enjoyed so much, that twenty-question thing. I mentally ticked off the list: Jack Bradfield, the woodpile, the box plants. (No, I'd already thought of the box plants.) Perhaps it was those pages of Marcel's letter? The hollow sofa? (Also ticked off.)

With a start, I knew. Stefan! Someone had rung, filled her in about us snogging in the sunken garden. I felt sick. I felt like running to the bathroom, sure the food I'd eaten was causing my queasiness. That darn taramasalata. The cod's roe was rising up. *Why hadn't I stuck to my raw vegan regime*? I gulped hard, fearing I was about to spew at my mother's feet.

I pushed the wisps from my French plait back in with wonky fingers, did my best to look her in the eye.

"*What* do you have to tell me?" she repeated.

Which sin should I pick? (I had a few to pick from.)

"Sorry, I forgot the clipping. I wrote it down, but—"

"That's not what I meant," she snapped.

I fiddled with the ragged bow at the end of my plait. A leaf fluttered to the ground.

"Where have you *been*, Genna?"

"The Becker's. Nowhere else, I swear." I tried to change the subject. "Where were you? I missed you."

"I was here, behaving like a lady."

So, was it suddenly ladylike to spend one's evening in sponge rollers?

"I asked *where have you been*?" Her face was puce.

"I told you. Dunno what else you want me to say."

A wilted petunia spilled to the floor. Then another. All the petunias began to drop until my torn top was exposed.

Namilly's face became seriously scary. "Look in the mirror. You looked drack when you left. Now you look like a whore. The lipstick, clothing, hair. Did you *enjoy* it?"

Ma was beside herself.

"Drack? I thought I looked cool when I left." I went trembly, determined to divert her thoughts away from Stefan. She tortured him enough, leaving him at the cyclone gate, making all those dog comments.

"*That*," she said, pointing at my jeans. "Who did that? There's only one way—"

"You're so wrong! I so did nothing."

"I knew the genes would out. You're becoming like her."

Her? Was Namilly talking about my birth mother?

"If you don't watch it, you'll end up the same." The words burst from her mouth.

So the sins of my birth mother were rising to haunt me? I didn't mind. There'd been too much skirting around the issue, secrets, lies. But how could I protest when I'd never seen her image, not the blurriest photo? I averted my gaze. What had my birth mother done to inspire such hatred in Ma?

"She had the morals of an alley cat, flaunting herself in the monokini, money, speeding on Promenade Roger Laroque."

Words flittered about me like dead leaves, but 'monokini' made my head jerk up. Where had I heard that before? My brain was foggy from too much champagne.

"I thought you said my birth mum worked for you?" I blurted.

"She did." Namilly's cheeks were flushed.

"But you just said she had money," I stammered. "Why would she, like, *work* for you?"

"She lost her money. And I couldn't have been happier."

My legs felt like jelly. "You're lying," I said. "None of this adds up."

A sponge roller bounded across the floor.

"Well, where do we go from here? Like I don't believe you. Like I don't believe any of this. Who am I, anyway?"

"A girl no one gave a hoot about until I came along. I saved you. We're a family now. I care far more than she ever did."

"You can't leave it like that. I need answers. I've been trawling the net, the agencies. Has my birth mother really passed away?"

Namilly nodded. I didn't believe her.

"How did she die?" I was grasping for more information. Apart from those trollop references, I still had nothing.

"She's no longer in your life. That's all you need to know."

Aggro things poured out of Namilly's mouth in French, argot I'd never heard before. She was unable to help herself. I resisted the urge to run to my room, and rake through the pages of my grammar book. I began to mumble verbs to calm myself.

"*Nounou*, please don't," I begged, unaware of what I'd said until I saw Namilly's face harden.

"Don't ever call me that. I won't tolerate it. I'll—"

"*You'll what?*" I yelled. "You'll put me in the hollow sofa, shut the lid down so I can hardly breathe. Push me against the white goose that hurt me and I still have dreams about?"

Her face froze.

I ploughed on. "And if I say my name is Geneviève, I get into *real* trouble. But you can't shut me in the hollow sofa anymore. I'm too old."

"Pull yourself together, Genna," she said calmly. "Why would I shut you in there? It's filled with my cans. There's no air, you would have suffocated."

Namilly was messing with my mind. She was right. I would've suffocated inside the hollow sofa.

"I suggest you clean up, go to bed. It's Christmas in the morning," she said, attempting to be oh-so-jolly. She turned, stomped off in a not-so-jolly fashion towards her bedroom.

Skye's safety pin was digging into me. The pain gave me strength. "You don't think I'm going to bed on my own? I'm going to find someone to sleep with, like my mother used to. I've never gone the whole way, and I plan to do something about it," I screamed at her receding back. "Anyway, you just don't get it."

But she was gone, and I felt like bawling.

I headed for the front door, hopping on one foot, and jamming my sandals back on. I rushed past the canna patch, and wheeled around the grevillea cubby. Hot tears ran down my cheeks.

I planned to head for the beach, and plunge into The Cauldron. No, I'd find myself a dinghy as Win had. Row out onto the Bay.

Chapter 46

Blobs of rain hit the ground, flicking up spurts of dirt and splattering my sandals. I knew I could no longer live with Namilly Perrier. I couldn't stand that chunky signet ring, her wiry hair, those grey skirts and trousers. Her safe shoes.

Vision blurred from crying, I swung around the curve in the road.

Outside the Winstone house, a police officer climbed into his car. The vehicle rolled off. Should I see if my friend was all right? I wondered. I hadn't spoken to her since she pumped her blowtorch at me. The outside light was still on. Would she be fizzed off if I knocked?

I took a breath, hauled open the gate.

The stubby grass made a scrunchy sound as I headed for the steps. I rapped on the front door. The shattered glass of the side panel was still covered in plastic. Win took her time to come to the door. She was fastening her bathrobe.

"You're back!" she said. She saw it was me, and frowned. "What do *you* want? Becker bash no good?"

"Neat enough," I sniffed. "Just wondering if everything's, you know, okay?"

"What makes you think it wouldn't be?"

"The cop car, I saw it drive off."

"Um, he's a friend. Drops by to check if I'm okay."

"Bit late for a social visit."

"Who are you? My mother?"

"Well," I said, not wanting to get into a brawl with Win, "I had a bingle with Ma. She dissed my birth mum. I'm planning to chuck it in."

"You'll be leaving home soon. So what's the big deal?"

"When I said *chuck* it in, I meant *end* it all in the Bay."

"Bit drastic, isn't it? Loyalty to your birth mum is great, but you don't even know her."

"I need your help," I hiccuped.

"Me? Help you? That's a laugh."

She began to close the door. Even the village weirdo didn't want to talk to me.

I turned to leave.

She opened the door again. "You're not serious about the Bay thing? Look, come in. Be quiet, though. Alice's had a bad evening. I've just got her to sleep. They so wander with this disease."

Had her policeman friend really just dropped by to check on her? Her eyes remained steady. Perhaps it was true.

I followed her into the hall. The horseshoe still lay there. We entered her kitchen with the primitive leaning stove.

"What've you been *doing*?" Her eyes raked my clothing. "You look a mess. Your jeans?" She gave me a sly smile.

"Why's everyone fussing over my jeans?"

"You sound like a cokehead."

"And *you* sound like Namilly." I surreptitiously eased my top down to cover my broken zipper.

"Well, p'raps she's right."

"It was Stefan."

"I don't need to know the gory details." She pointed at my jeans again. "Did you have it off with him?"

"Nup, didn't happen."

"You trying to tell me you've never *done* it with him before?"

I shook my head, fiddled with my French plait. Another leaf fell to the floor. (I seemed to be carrying a whole garden around on my body that night.)

"Mind you, I don't know how you can stand to touch him. Not with all that facial stuff happening."

"He's been on cortisone, Win," I said, feeling fuzzy. "He looked *great* tonight, like Kurt Cobain, a total spunk. Hot. Had lover's ooh … ooh … ouch, though."

"What's that, Gen?"

"Dunno. Some sort of male condition."

"Can it be cured?" She looked interested.

"Dunno."

"And this mysterious condition caused him to try to rape you. Torn top? Did he do that?"

"Nup, tore it myself to make it look sexier, to compete with those turtle chests like Elizabeth." I ran my tongue over my teeth, furry from Stefan's tsatsiki kiss.

"You're seriously weird," she said. "I'm not surprised Namilly was shirty."

"Why? What's wrong with the way I look?" I was starting to get annoyed.

"Purple lippy, torn fingernail, torn top. Safety pins. Something strange about your eyebrow. What's going on?"

"Everything burst in the sunken garden."

"I can see that," she said dryly. "You look like a grade-A skank."

"The oldies liked the way I look. Vince Becker, Joe Stubbs. It was revolting. And they never even glanced at me before."

Win twisted her fingers through her tousled hair, and suppressed a yawn.

"Ma was more than angry." I couldn't wait to tell her the truth. "She said my birth mother was a tart."

"Well, she should know. Your birth mother used to work for her."

"She said she had money, drove fast cars. It doesn't add up."

Win looked as if she knew something, but was not about to tell me. "Never heard anything about that. Sure you're not imagining it?"

I decided to plunge right in. "She lies, that's what I can't stand. Smells of pee and antiseptic, doesn't tell me what's going on. *Then* I find out about Alice's Korsa-whatsit disease." I joggled my finger at her. "You *both* lied."

"We've been over that. I didn't lie. It was all in your mind. Anyway, your mother was protecting me." Win nodded. "She's looked after us on and off for a while now. She was cleaning Mum up after a binge when

Dad walked in. I guess he took it the wrong way." Her mouth formed an O. "He racked off."

I considered asking if it was the 'situation' she'd referred to as she jabbed me with her blowtorch, but changed my mind. "Well, how about this for a whopper," I said, sticking out my jaw, "slab of misinformation. You had a phone installed lately?"

Win shook her head.

"So there you go, prime example. She said you rang while I was out."

"Maybe Korsakoff's is catching. Like a tisane?" She pushed herself up, ran water into the stained electric jug which rattled as it spewed out steam. "Erksy stuff." She held up a pale packet. "It's all I drink now."

"Good thing, too."

She dunked two sachets of camomile into the chipped floral mugs. "You'll be pleased to know I'm off the scent. SSRIs, instead. By court order. Night you came, I mixed in a bit of vodka to give it a boost. Sort of like a floral martini."

"Dis-gusting!" Was Namilly supplying Win with Stoli, as well? Surely not. "Where'd you get it?" I felt myself tense up.

"At the Bottle Shop." She handed me my hippie tea. "I am eighteen, y'know."

"Did you really mean to harm me?"

"Yep, I thought I'd rearrange your pretty face."

I hesitated. "And Hank?"

"Don't even think about it. He's not worth the brain space."

Things between us had just upped a notch. "I feel better now."

"Why? Because I said I would've hurt you?"

"Nope, 'cos this gross drink is settling my stomach. The cod's roe in the taramasalata dip made me sick as a dog. I was planning to throw up, but I bumped into Stefan."

Win did the lip-pursing thing. "I think you've got a problem."

"What sort of problem?"

"Bulimia, ever thought about it?"

"It's not a disease. I'm raw vegan."

"Well, I'm telling you—" A scuffling sound on the staircase.

Alice Winstone appeared, like a crumpled ghost. "Is there any coffee?" she quavered.

Win got up. "Like a cup, Mum?"

She hauled open the door labelled MUGS, and extracted a mug covered in peach-coloured bees and flowers and crimson butterflies. She placed a used sachet inside, poured hot water over it, and gave it a diffident dunk.

She sat Alice down, and handed it to her.

Her mother slurped contentedly. "Mmm, nice drink." Liquid dribbled down her chin. "Very nice coffee."

Win's face was Buddha-like.

"Hello Namilly's daughter." Alice's faded eyes stared at me.

So, Alice had recognised me again. Was her memory being jogged by all those flowers Namilly believed had recuperative properties?

"I had an argument with Namilly tonight," I confided.

"With whom?" There was fear in her eyes.

"Your friend, Namilly."

"I don't know anyone called Namilly." Alice gave a stubborn shake of the head.

"But I've seen you with her."

Win was making negative signs at me with her hands. I stopped rabbiting on about my mother.

"When did you get back from China, dear?" Her voice was querulous.

"This morning." I was getting used to these freaky conversations.

"I'm glad." Saliva hung from her lip. "Is that geisha lipstick?" She pointed to my purple mouth.

"You're confabulating, Mum, wrong country." Win placed her hand under Alice's elbow, and eased her from the chair. "Back to bed now."

I heard them slowly mount the stairs, heard Win coax Alice as if she were a difficult kid.

My friend became an instant heroine that night. I forgave her for everything as I gazed around her kitchen, and watched cockroaches sleazing in the corners. Was this the sort of place I'd be living in if I left?

"I've changed my mind about ending it on the Bay. I'll hitchhike to Melbourne tonight," I said when Win returned. The washing machine churned in the distance.

"No way. You won't leave *ever*, Gen." She pointed a work-worn finger at me. The main bearing began to roar. "Face it, you'll hang around like a bad smell. Why? 'Cos Namilly's got the key to your past. You'll *never* let go."

"It's all very well for you. You know who your birth mother is. You're lucky."

"That's a laugh! But you're right. I am lucky. She hit me over the head for my own good. How many mothers'd do that?" She gave a soft giggle.

Win opened a drawer marked ODDS AND ENDS. Extracted a small book, and tossed it to me.

"Read this, before you do anything. It's a Legal Aid thing."

Am I Old Enough? was a small red book with an image of a girl on the cover.

"Your rights. And you might think twice about smoking those chop-chop rollies."

The page fell open at Police Questioning. "Seventeen years and over," I read aloud. "You do not have to give police an *intimate body sample.*"

"It's all right, he's married," she grinned. "Now turn to the passport page. You can't get one in your own name until you're eighteen without parental consent. Means I can, you can't. Ironic, isn't it? I don't need one, you will."

I took Win's advice. I went home that night instead of ending it all in the waters of Port Phillip Bay. Bill Einstein snuffled and flicked as I left, hooted steam high into the air.

Behind me, an upstairs window flew up. "Stick with it, kid," Win shouted, before slamming the sash down.

Lightning bleached the Bay. Rain sheeted crossways. I dawdled up the road, not bothered about being drenched. Just bothered about Namilly.

Chapter 47

How dare you desecrate Jane's special place. Wog slag!

Elizabeth Stubbs' message greeted me on Christmas morning when I booted up. She'd emerged from her personality-free zone, turned e-bully, and proved she wasn't totally brain dead by admitting how she felt about me. But 'Jane's special place' had me scratching my head. The sunken garden had been a 'remorse gift' from Vince to Jane for his having cracked onto the chick behind the register. Had it become a *shrine* or something?

Happy Christmas to you too, Fat Betty! With a click of the Delete button, I dispatched her warped thoughts to the rubbish bin.

Through the spam and screen waviness a message from Elise crept across the screen. She asked if we could meet. Would Elise be like Jules, older than she claimed? I'd think about it.

Receiving mail ... flashed next. It was Marcel, wishing me *Joyeux Noël*, telling me he'd sent a letter by snail mail. Why did he always correspond twice? Did he not trust Namilly?

The air was awash with aggression. I decided to head for the beach. I left a surrender candle, white and unwrapped, for Namilly on the mantelpiece—a false gesture of reconciliation. Win was right. I would never cut off the last line to my identity. But I was glad the Ulysses butterfly had been destroyed by Jack Bradfield. It would've been inappropriate after those things Namilly'd said.

The sand was sloppy, the beach deserted, the sky overcast. Not a boat, not a seagull in sight. It was as though the entire town was recovering from a massive hangover. The bathing boxes were locked, even the Rasmussen blue one.

I ambled to the rocks beneath Ti Point, hoping Stefan would be there. I wanted to explain, say something that would bring us together again. "Stick with it, kid," Win'd shouted. I would've been happy if he just forgave me for losing his anklet.

Under the overhang of the cliff, close to the churning Cauldron, I found a flat rock, as hard as the interior of our hollow sofa. After the argument with Namilly, I was certain she'd used the sofa as a disciplinary tool. I remembered the weeping, the yelling, the fear as I pushed against the lid. The silence from the other side.

But there was something more, something niggling at my subconscious: occasional hushed talking, a rocking motion, a slapping sound. A ship sound, creaking, the smell of diesel.

I recalled running my finger along the beak of the white ceramic goose. I even recalled its name: Doudou. And Doudou was the coldest security blanket in the universe. The keeping of the cans came later, probably when Alice fell ill.

Namilly's logic was bulletproof. Hollow sofas were airless. I would've died. So why did I remember light? Pale, filtered light. Was there a fissure, a gap of some sort? Something in the framework that let the rays shine in?

There'd been no kisses better, no cuddles to make things right. Just that word—*Nounou*. Just her coldness. When had these episodes ended? When I was fit for everyone to see, fit for the people of Ravella to prod and poke and say hi to? Or had the keeping of the cans saved me?

I was blown away thinking about these things.

A movement in the rock pool distracted me. A ripple of water, a flutter. A small creature swayed, floated and hung, as if in space, blending with the sandy bottom. Was it a blue ringer?

I scrambled for a piece of driftwood, poked the medusa in the belly until it lit up like a disco dancer. The blue ringer flung and twitched, turned fizzy citron and strutted its stuff—a bit like Angela in her day-glo tube dress. Then erupted into a symphony of blue rings, glittering against the yellow. It writhed and twisted, powerless until swept away by the following tide.

I laughed as I watched, leaning this way and that to avoid the toxic spit of the octopus. A pair of thongs blurred up beside me. Stefan'd come to join in the fun.

"Look, Stef. It's fantabulous. Dudical. Sit down." I patted an adjacent rock.

He didn't reply. I looked up. No one was there, only some seaweed.

The colours faded. The blue ringer blended back into the silt and the salt until it was almost transparent again. I looked at my watch. Time to face the music. That was, if Namilly was even talking to me. And I planned to boot up, work out my next move in the hunt for my roots.

I trudged along the sand, and struggled up the ragged path. From the top of the cliff, a muffled wisp of smoke caught my eye. Elizabeth, crouched behind the Becker bathing box, choofed on a chop-chop rollie. Her jellies gleamed in the gloom of the overhang. My heart did a lurch thing. Fat Betty was seriously stalking Stefan.

I saw a floppy hat in the distance. A mountain of zinc cream walked in my direction. I gave an arm-ripping wave.

He turned and disappeared.

A whole ant farm began to rattle around inside my stomach. Followed by a whoosh of envy. Had that kiss beneath the mistletoe turned Elizabeth into an instant dudette?

Had she and Stefan arranged to meet?

Chapter 48

Two days later, I discovered Marcel's letter balanced between the tendrils of the banana passion fruit, halfway up the side of the house.

Namilly was in the garden tying back an overgrown jasmine. Had the postman been guzzling his Christmas gifts? Or had she placed the letter there, planning to bury it later? (Our relationship was in the zilch zone, conversation reduced to grunts and snubs since the Becker bash.)

Black worms crawled across the letter's surface.

I brushed the worms off, went to my kitchen, grabbed a handful of *raisins secs* from the Tupperware container, and sauntered to my room to read in private.

I is staying at place called Amédée Apartments, Arlington Esplanade— big name for not so big street. It is very wet, raining frogs and cats. I miss Nouméa. I miss my boat—he is called Marguerite. I miss kava from nakamal in Baie des Citrons (relaxing to do this). I miss gun for shooting deer and Notou bird in Brousse. I miss all things, really. As you see, I have very much homesick.

I licked my finger. Whatever was a Notou bird?

Coral Sea break on sand and shore metres from my window. Is like big, silver cord connecting me to my homeland. The building is ugly. There is dolphins and tropical fish and all sorts of crazy things running on top of walls. Fish, fish, fish. Everywhere fish. We not do this in Nouméa. Is not chic. (Aquarium is place for fish; lovely aquarium at Anse Vata.) The fish is even on curtains. There is lumps of coral everywhere, on coffee table, in bathroom. A hairy coconut is door stop and I keep hurting my foots when I bump into her. But is nice to be in naked foots. I even buy thongs. (Shoes too hot. Anyway, thongs much less dear here.)

But I very excited. I meet crocodile on beach!

Wow! Even *I'd* never seen a crocodile outside of the zoo. I chewed hard on my raisins.

I explain. I see man searching old wedding rings in sand with metal detector. Crocodile jump out of bushes and try to chop off his leg. I pick up stick and help him fighting this beast. And we win!!! We poke crocodile in eye and he run back in the dirty water. (Water very dirty up here, not as clean as in my country. No lovely lagoon. Lagoon is biggest in world. Have I tell you this?)

They smoke much dope in Management Apartment. It is right under me, on ground floor. It remind me of when I am student, many years ago.

Have you had postcard from me, green fish in their volcanic lake home in Tableland on the front? The green fish cause me to think of you.

I stopped reading. He'd sent a postcard. Had Namilly buried it beneath the Norfolk Island pine before I could see it? And he said I reminded him of GREEN FISH. I knew I was olive-skinned. But, *green*? I swallowed the last of my sundried *raisin secs*, skimmed through the remainder of his letter:

I come back in Ravella, after I receive result of tests. Will you meet me at house on Ti Point? I send you time and date from email. We have much to discuss. (Everything depend on tests.) *Bisous*, Marcel.

The letter fluttered to the floor. What tests was Marcel talking about? Were they connected to his smoking Gauloises Blondes? (I recalled tell-ing him to switch to chop-chop—the bleach occasionally spoiled the flavour, but it quickly passed through the gut, sort of like tap water.) At last I understood the reason for Marcel to be constantly travelling to Cairns. There was a large hospital up there. And maybe a well-known oncologist in residence. A bad feeling loomed.

Marcel had said his father died of lung cancer, and soapy pipe tobacco in cigarette paper was a disaster waiting to happen. Was that the reason his hair was so thin? Had he been on chemo before I met him? I was in a tizzy. A rash of goose bumps decorated my arms.

Then again, there could be other reasons for Marcel to undergo medical treatment. His wrestle with the crocodile? Perhaps he'd been injured, his injury turning to gangrene. And he *had* been seated on the day he offered me the toe ring. Looked wrung out, as well. (D'oh! I was starting to get confused—that toe ring episode had happened well before the crocodile attack.)

A shiver whipped through me. Had Marcel had his leg cut off? Would he be using a walking stick when I saw him next? A one-legged Marcel would be totally feral. Had he written to Skye, told her about these tests? She'd been a nursing aide before she became a laundry consultant at Last Gasp Guesthouse. Would he take her back to Noumea so she could nurse him? I wondered whether I could help. I'd fixed up Alice without gagging. I'd be happy to do the same for him if it came to the crunch.

I quivered and sweated, fretting about his condition. All sorts of reasons for the tests came to mind. I knew I wouldn't sleep a wink until I saw him next.

Screwing his letter into a tight ball, I hurried to the oak armoire near the front entrance. I squeezed it into the scanty space between the fur-niture and the wall. These might be his last words, all I had left of him. I'd be fizzed off if I lost them.

I creaked open the door of the armoire to check its stability. A gust of foetid air revealed Namilly's battered Louis Vuitton suitcase. Her gar-dening shoes, caked in mud, were lined up like soldiers from the Great War. Above the shoes hung a raincoat in cracked plastic, but not much else. Unlike the hollow sofa, the armoire was pretty much ignored. Namilly would never think to look behind it.

I closed the door again. Pressed my body flat. Squinted. I was unable to see Marcel's letter. No way would Namilly discover it. I could smell curry cooking in her sunroom kitchen.

My hands were wimping out. I was seriously stressed. I needed to grind myself a vegetable drink.

I pulled out the juicer, jammed fruit and vegetables into the feed chute, using a ginormous amount of natural produce. I poked in organic apples, hand-picked bananas, fertilizer-free carrots, sun-ripened cucumbers, hydroponic broccoli and a piece of cauliflower, whose mould I scraped off with my fingernail. I added fresh gnarled ginger for energy, a raw spud for vitamin C, after removing the eyes and cutting away the rotted bits.

The machine churned and trembled, shook, sprayed sawdust over my safety specs. I skolled the thick green drink straight from the jug.

The juice made no difference.

I still felt edgy about Marcel's letter.

Chapter 49

There was a call from The Store. The shelf-stacking job was delayed an extra week. Arch Biddle had deferred his holidays. So I read, took long walks on the beach. The days dragged by slowly.

Elise began pounding me with emails. I was tempted to meet her. She sent a message asking me to join her at Pedro's coffee shop in Kingston. Was her choice of meeting place a coincidence? Or was Jules contacting me, this time under a different name?

I decided to stay away from chat rooms for a while.

Win'd gone to ground again, with Alice indoors due to the bone-chillingly drizzly weather. The waves surged over The Cauldron, crashing onto the rocks beneath Ti Point. I was fractious and fidgety, fed up with windy walks. I waited for the postman each day, hoping for Marcel's fish card to arrive. There was no sign of it.

Every day, Namilly dug in the garden like a manic mole. She wore clear PVC, a matching plastic scarf over her spiky hair. She said the damp soil made the weeds fly out. Even the miasma from her cans was subdued. It was as if the flies had flown to a warmer place.

New Year's Eve passed almost unnoticed. Still no Stefan on the other side of the gate. I checked often, but he was never there. He did not return my calls. I began to be concerned about his health. Had he told me the full story about those cortisone injections? Were they hormonal, or something worse? What with Marcel and his lungs and legs, plus Stefan and his cortisone, I was antsy.

I prayed, sucked up to the big guy in the sky. Said I'd quit searching for my birth mother if Stefan and Marcel turned out to be all right.

I spot-cleaned the surface of my quilt to pass the time. Made by the Amish, had it come from the USA during the American wartime occupation of New Caledonia? Had Namilly purchased it from a stall in Anse Vata at one of the Thursday markets? I wondered.

Bored with quilt cleaning, I turned my attention to other things. I found so much stuff. Old exam papers. Muesli bar wrappers. Keys which didn't fit any lock whatsoever. Melted Bic pens with teeth marks on the end. Rusted glider clips. Lipsticks with lost tops. A card of fat plastic hair bows, rainbow coloured. A red thong for my right foot. Puckered bubblegum with dead ants stuck to its surface.

Legs crossed, I sat there wondering about the bubblegum. What caused the ants to die? I smoothed out the wrapper. No NGM on the label. No wonder I felt icky so often. I wondered if I should complain, write to somebody.

Next, I examined the joggers I'd worn on the night of Win's blow-torch war. Mould surrounded the tears in the canvas where Alice's dinner had seeped through. I decided to wash them. They were my comfort footwear. The tears on the toes acted like air-conditioning. I jammed my hand into the left foot to keep the canvas firm while I scrubbed with a nailbrush. I felt an object inside, a wedge of some sort, like paper screwed up. Much as I'd done with Marcel's latest letter.

Uh-oh, had Namilly found his letter already, shoved it in my shoe, planning to bury it in the garden?

I yanked the lump with my fingers, and jerked it free. I was holding crumpled fifties. I smoothed the money out. Were these the notes I'd lost, the ones I could've sworn I'd placed in my leopard-print G-string? At no time had they been in my jogger. So what was the money doing there? Had Namilly done this?

I stormed out of the house. Marched towards the row of lilacs where she was up to her ears in mud and wriggling earthworms.

"You stole my money!" I yelled, jogger in one hand, creased fifties in the other.

"What?" She jumped back, water streaming down her see-through scarf. "Whose money is that? Mine?"

"No, it's mine. You stole it!"

"If I stole it, how come you've got it? You're as silly as Alice." She picked up her bone-handled knife, and wiggled out a weed.

"Then how come it *happened* to turn up in my joggers?"

"Aren't you the lucky one," she cooed. "I wish someone would leave money in *my* shoes. Perhaps it was the tooth fairy. Or the toe fairy, I should say?" She threw down the bone-handled knife, picked up a shovel, and jammed it under a clod with her foot.

I stood there trembling with anger.

The rain was zigzagging down the notes like crazy. I could see I was getting nowhere. Namilly wasn't about to fess up as she had when she buried those pages of Marcel's letter.

"I borrowed it," Namilly shouted at my back as I hurried off. "You should be more careful where you leave your things. Leopard-print G-strings invite investigation."

"So you *did* lie," I screamed at her. "You *did* steal my hair money. That so sucks."

"Everybody lies." She shrugged and went back to her weeds.

Bent over, Namilly seemed thinner. Almost fragile. Was Alice's problem eating away at my mother, too? Was *that* disease catching? I began to wonder what it must be like to see someone dying before your eyes, not knowing you anymore. Would it be the same with Marcel? Worst of all, was Stefan's skin condition more than psoriasis and sunburn?

The thought of mortality was starting to scare me.

There was one bright star. I'd found my money. I'd have my hair done especially for Marcel. I would catch a bus to Kingston, arrange to meet Elise afterwards. At Pedro's coffee shop.

I decided to email her, tell her to wear a gold hoop earring in one ear. A humungous one. (That'd soon sort out if Jules was part of the equation.) We'd have a heart-to-heart about our birth mother research.

I placed my joggers down to dry. Booted up. Typed out my message to Elise. Pressed Send. *Receiving mail ...* flashed back. An incoming email:

10 am tomorrow, Ti Point house, Marcel.

I'd be forced to cancel my meeting with Elise. I would have my hair done by Sophie Pfeiffer on the highway.

Chapter 50

I thrashed my way through another sofa dream. Namilly held down the lid while I shrieked to be free. I yelled, hammered and bashed the white goose against her face. The goose morphed into a dust covered bag of sugared almonds.

☆ ☆ ☆

Waking in a lather of sweat, I glanced at the clock. I'd slept through the alarm. The phone rang. I left it and hotfooted to the bathroom.

The house was quiet. I detected no smells of bacon and eggs, no burning waffles from the sunroom kitchen.

The box of matches beside the gas heater was soggy. I used up the entire box in a fruitless effort to get one to strike. So I shivered under tepid water. While smoothing a soap bar over my body, I discovered a bruise on my hip shaped like a vampire's kiss—livid lips, with a green tongue inside. Had the sofa dream caused that?

I patted myself dry, stepped into my leopard-print G-string and dragged on my second best jeans, carefully pressed the night before. (My best ones were a lost cause since the sunken garden.)

I pulled a clean white T-shirt over my head, and slid my feet into a pair of new black thongs with hot-pink soles. I felt tense, not only about Marcel Manet's health, but because I'd never been invited to the house on Ti Point in an official capacity before. (My visits had always been sneaky—like the time Win was blown out to sea and I snooped among Marcel's things, came across the photo of that mysterious couple propped beside his whisky.) I didn't have to worry about plaiting my hair. Sophie Pfeiffer could do it after she'd finished the cutting.

After squirting myself with the remainder of last year's Miss Dior perfume, I applied a touch of lipstick in tasteful pink. (I dreaded meeting Marcel. It was sure to be yuck.) I stuffed a fifty in my pocket, grabbed my keys, and hurried through the living room on my way to the front door.

The fire was out, even though the day was cool. Namilly must've gone to help Alice, I reasoned. Then again, the silence in the house felt different, a sort of emptiness.

I grabbed a banana passionfruit, and slammed the cyclone wire gate shut behind me.

Choosing not to cut through the ti-trees for fear of bumping into Hank or Jack Bradfield, I walked along the side of the road. I glanced at my watch. Almost half-past eight. I would have to hitch a lift, or I'd be late for my appointment.

With my hair clinging in wet wisps to my face, I waved down a passing car. A trembling bucket of bolts pulled up with a race and cough. I ran to it, hauled open the door. Uh-oh, I spied two bulging eyes: Joe Stubbs.

I began to back away.

"Don't be silly, girl. I won't rape you," he rasped.

I slid in beside him, heart racing in time with the vehicle. "Store, please," I squeaked.

He pressed his foot down hard on the accelerator. The radio blasted: *Uptown girl.* Clumpy hands clamped the steering wheel. I eyed those hands warily. Would they unclamp, wander across the sticky vinyl towards me? Pinch me again? His wedding band was thick and yellow. What a hypocrite he was. Had he and Florence had words after the Becker bash? That evening made me cringe whenever I thought about it.

"Going to work?" I asked. (Stubbs' Bodyworks was a short walk from the Becker service station.)

Joe grunted.

"Not on holidays yet?"

No reply.

I decided to try him on the subject of his daughter. "Elizabeth, um, well?"

He grunted again.

I took a breath. "Bringing home the bacon?"

He sniffed.

Then it dawned on me—Joe Stubbs, father of Fat Betty, had *no idea* who I was. Not a flicker of recognition now I was no longer wearing my torn black top and tight jeans. He probably didn't even recall having pinched me.

We pulled up at The Store and I climbed out, feeling very Plain Jane. I thanked him, waving my Percy-shaped fruit in a farewell gesture.

I almost tripped over Jason Bjorkman and Angela Rasmussen playing mouth to mouth with a musk stick on the pavement. I scooted past, head down, hoping they wouldn't notice—not that they could've smiled even if they'd wanted to.

Sophie Pfeiffer's home was painted in icing pink. Micro fairy lights were strung around the windows. (Uncool Ravella parents said she sold haircuts in the daytime, her body at night.) But she was cheap, cheerful and convenient.

Inside was chaos. Dirty dishes, food scraps, kids shrieking and running around waving Vegemite toast.

"Sorry, love," Sophie said, pushing back her stringy blonde hair, "but holidays drive me demented."

An androgynous ankle biter in denim overalls cycled around the linoleum. The television blared. Feral kids barrelled in and out of doors. No one had ever sighted a husband or partner. Did Sophie's children pound her with questions about their identity?

"Come into the bathroom, love. It's all set up in there."

She sat me on a tubular chair and closed the door. The war on the other side hummed on, a distant distraction. Were they killing one another? Sophie didn't seem to care.

"How many do you have?" I asked, as she damped my already damp hair.

She began to snip. "Four, love." I began to relax. Locks landed on the floor around me. "Plus one niece. They won't *really* murder each other. Just sounds like it. Goin' out tonight?"

I shook my head. "Can you fix the plait?"

Her weaving was schmick. I was glad to let someone else do the hard yakka. She wound an elastic band around the end. I examined my reflection.

"Those short bits around my face, what'll I do with those?" I indicated the hair hanging over my eyes. I resembled an English sheepdog.

"Hair clips. Pretty ones, but. Not skanky, though."

I remembered the fat plastic bows I'd thrown away. "Too kiddy," I said. "I need to look mature."

Would I tell her about Marcel?

"I have a meeting with a friend, about a will. Actually, he's unwell and in pain. I need a more adult style." I swept the air with my hands. "He might leave me his yacht."

"Really, love? A yacht? I'll curl the fringe then." Sophie lunged for the tongs on the bench. She plugged them into a grubby socket. "It'll take away the schoolmarm thing."

"Schoolmarm thing?"

"Yeah, the frumpsville 'do you were wearing."

"I thought my hair was, um, you know, elegant."

Sophie grabbed my hair. She began to wind it around her hot rod. It smelled as though a bushfire had broken out in the room. A great frizz erupted. My fringe, still over my eyes, looked as if she'd rammed my fingers into the socket.

She saw my glum expression. "It'll wash out, love. Not like a permanent you're stuck with."

I pulled fifty dollars from my pocket.

"Your nails are nude," she said.

Ignoring the sales pitch I grabbed the change from her fuchsia fingers, sidestepped a soggy rusk and exited her front door clutching my uneaten banana passionfruit.

A man stood on the other side of the highway, propped near a stand of gum trees along from the Zabaglione Woollen Shop. He was clad in beige shorts and walk socks, and wore a gold earring in his left ear. Although clean shaven, he was a dead ringer for the guy who'd asked me to meet him at Pedro's coffee shop in Kingston: Jules.

My heart did a doom dive. I'd told *Elise* to wear a gold earring. *Not* Jules. Were Jules and Elise the same person? If so, would he recognise me? I flicked the frizzy fringe over my left eye as camouflage.

Too wussy to use the short cut through the ti-tree bushes, I hurried down Ravella Crescent. Praying Jules would not follow.

Chapter 51

Stefan and I nearly collided.

I was powering along in my new thongs, my mind on the guy standing near the Zabaglione Woollen Shop, when a mountain of white—white cap, white towel, white T-shirt, white shorts, white zinc cream—confronted me.

"Slow down, mate. You'll bust a gasket!" Stefan clutched a clear cliplock bag containing an empty Coke can.

"Stef! What's that?" I felt myself flush.

"Electrified medusa in a can."

"I won't even *ask* what you're planning to do with it."

Silence descended over the two of us like an awkward cone.

"How've you been?" we both began at the same time.

"You haven't been around." I quavered, not daring to ask him about Fat Betty.

"Slaving at the service station," he said. "The old man's ticker's a bit dicky. Anyway, you've been sick."

I felt a surge of jealousy at the thought of him working shoulder to shoulder with the cashier chick, worse even than when I saw him kissing Elizabeth.

"Whaddya mean I've been sick?"

"You're mong of a … called out. Informed me from the flower bed."

"Oh, she's just pissed 'cos of Christmas Eve."

"You tell 'er?" His eyes looked flustered.

"Don't be a dork. It was, like, you know, my clothing. She wasn't hiding behind a bush or anything."

I could feel myself grow hot. I saw the rising blush beneath his zinc cream and decided to change the subject.

"Like my new hairdo?" I swivelled my head to the side and back.

"Looks weird." I could see he was fixated with the frizzy fringe flopping across my left eye.

"Um, she said it was less frumpsville."

"Who did?"

"Sophie Pfeiffer on the highway."

My excitement at seeing Stefan was subsiding. I remembered his injection. "Had any, um, more of those, you know, cortisone shots?" Although, beneath the layer of protective pap, it was obvious his skin had returned to its former condition.

He shook his head. I handed him my uneaten banana passionfruit. "Eat this. It's raw vegan, good for you." I touched his face.

I looked at my watch. I'd be late for my meeting if I didn't get a move on.

"Well, hope Vince gets better so he can, you know."

"What?"

"Do the cashier chick again."

"Oh, get fucked!" Stefan stormed off.

I was so happy I wanted to laugh out loud. We were mates once more. "I love you," I called out.

He hesitated. The back of his ears grew earnest.

"I love you very much," I shouted.

"Oh, get lost!"

He turned, and I could see his grin—yellow cheese surrounded by white chalk. He disappeared, still grasping the banana passionfruit.

I headed for the house on Ti Point, my spirits soaring. Stefan and I were back together again. Perhaps, one day, I *would* like to be the wife of a service station proprietor.

Mrs B of BP? Sounded kinda cool. And if Marcel Manet *did* leave me the Marguerite in his will, we could sail around the world together, collecting blue ringers as we went.

Chapter 52

I lifted the brass circle from the mouth of the lion, and banged it. While waiting for Marcel to answer my knock I ran my finger over my upper lip.

My palm was strangely sticky. I smoothed my hand over my jeans. Would Marcel have changed since I last saw him? Would there be obvious signs of his illness? Then again, perhaps those tests had been negative.

I had a thought: Skye Becker might be there. I couldn't *face* seeing Skye again, with her sexually liberated arrogance. *Sooo* embarrassing, I told myself.

I turned to leave.

The door opened. *"Bonjour!"*

Marcel's Blanc Bleu shirt was immaculate. His boat shoes were spotless. You could've used the crease in his powder-blue trousers for cutlery. I gazed at those pants—no man in Ravella would've been seen dead in duds like that. Way too slick.

Then it sank in. I could see no crutch or walking stick. *Marcel had two legs.* (Unless he was wearing a prosthesis? Which could've been the reason for him wearing those daggy slacks.)

"Ça va?" he asked. His face was evenly tanned.

"Ça va," I replied. "I'm okay."

He gave me two kisses in the French manner.

My heart paddled fast as I followed him into the room with the faded turquoise carpet.

"Skye late?" I murmured.

He didn't reply. He pointed to a balloon-backed chair.

I repeated my question. "Skye Becker late?" I curled my toes. "She coming as well?"

He hesitated, and then shook his head. "Would you like a drink? Coke in fridge, some fizzy sing as well. I cannot remember 'is name."

"No thanks." I didn't want to look like some gumby kid sucking on a fizzy drink in front of Marcel.

He unscrewed his bottle of Jack Daniel's, splashed some into a glass and began to sip. The photo of the couple leaning against the Mercedes was still there.

"Well, zere is things I must explain."

He sat down opposite, lifted the knees of his trousers with his thumb and forefinger. I observed hairy legs, ruling out my prosthesis theory. (One worry I was able to cross off my list.) His eyes fixed themselves on my face.

"You 'ave somesing white." He pointed to my upper lip.

I ran the back of my hand across my mouth, and saw zinc cream.

"Sorry, it's bits of Stefan," I said.

My eyes latched onto a splodge on my jeans. I decided not to touch it.

"Ze eyebrow?" Marcel pointed again.

I was becoming flustered by his interest in my face. "The burnt eyebrow, it happened when the gas heater exploded before the Becker bash. It's my new hairdo highlighting it, you know the floppy fringe to the side. You see, I found your money. And I went to Sophie on the highway—"

Marcel began to cough. He grew purple. He rose from his chair, went to the window and turned the handle. He pushed open the pane, and blew his nose on a bright yellow handkerchief.

I remembered the tests. "Are your lungs okay?"

"*Merci*, zey is now." He cleared his throat, and sat down again. "Ze tests. I 'ave results, and you must know—"

"The *Marguerite*!" I gasped.

"*Marguerite qui?*" He looked puzzled.

"Your yacht."

"What is my yacht to do wis tests?"

I began to feel embarrassed that I was hoping to get rich from his illness. "It's your feet, I mean, the problems caused by changing sails, rushing about going downwind, upwind. Whatever."

I knew zip about sailing.

"My foots is very well," he said.

"Those thongs, did they help?"

He raised an eyebrow.

"You know, those flip-flops you said you bought."

"Very good, very cheap." Marcel made a dismissive motion. "I 'ave results of tests—"

"Is it a heart condition?" My own was doing jungle drums.

"Mademoiselle, I will 'ave *crise cardiaque* if you not let me finish."

"Sorry. What did the tests show?"

"Tests show you is ze one."

"What one?" What had *I* to do with Marcel's health?

"You are baby of Sandrine Bas Salaire de Lyon."

His words seemed far off. The mullioned windows began to whirl, went black and grey and white in sparkling prisms. The room blurred in a crazy play of light. A screwdriver was skewering through my stomach. How could Sandrine be my birth mother? What about all those people on the net who'd been helping me in my search? They hadn't discovered a thing. None of this made sense.

"I thought you were sick," I cried. "I worried about your health so much, I lost sleep."

"I is well," he said. "Tests were of ADN."

"ADN?"

"I is sorry." He licked his lips. "In English, you say DNA. You match wis Sandrine."

"But there was no swab, no blood sample taken."

Marcel reached across. He touched my frizzy fringe, and gave it a gentle yank.

"You never *touched* me," I cried.

And then I recalled his pulling my French plait, squeezing my shoulder on the day he gave me the toe ring.

"So *that's* why you gave me that gift?"

His face was expressionless.

"How *dare* you come here interfering in my business. You and your yucky clothes."

"What is wrong wis my clothes?" He glanced at his trousers.

"They're slick. They're spivvy. They're foreign."

"Foreign? You is right. I buy my clothes in Paris."

"And they're tacky, too." I could feel my eyes well up.

I fought back the tears. It seemed I'd been told the names of my natural parents. But how did I know it was true? How did I know he was more honest than those dodgy people like Jules?

"You, you *Caldoche*. You've made my life difficult. *I worried about you*, and I needn't have bothered. Not to *mention* that phone call asking me to meet you in Cairns." My throat was dry.

"Madame Perrier tell you I ring?"

"I overheard her talking to you, and it set her off. She called me a tramp. She said I was like my mother, a skank."

"Perhaps it true." A smile tweaked at the corner of his mouth.

"Did she ever work for Namilly, Sandrine I mean?"

"*Non*, but she work much now. She run Amédée Apartments in beaches close to Cairns."

So the *real* reason Marcel had gone to Cairns was to see Sandrine? I began to tremble. My teeth chattered. My stomach churned. I was hungry and confused, and I'd eaten nothing that morning, not even a banana passionfruit. Was Jack Daniel's raw vegan? I wondered.

"Can I have some of your whisky?"

Marcel looked doubtful.

"I'm almost eighteen, just a few months down the track."

"Your muzzer say—"

"Yeah, I heard her on the phone. She said I'm beneath the age of consent. Well, that's garbage. She knows how old I am. And I'm nearly old enough to buy my own grog."

I gulped down the drink he gave me. The whisky burned its way through, until my body began to glow.

"Well, what's Sandrine say about all this?"

"I not tell 'er. I work for Sandrine's papa, Jacques Forestier. Zey not talk."

"How'd you get a piece of *her* hair?"

"Oh, much butts around pool. I got, 'ow you say—pissed—and after I fighted with crocodile, I touch 'er."

"Did you buy *her* off with a toe ring, too?" I spat.

He did not reply.

I pushed my uncool hairdo from my eyes with shaky fingers. "That her?" I pointed to the photo on the walnut table.

He handed it to me.

"She still beautiful?" I examined the couple.

"*Oui*, still beautiful. But skin much damaged from sun."

I saw Marcel's eyes light upon the soles of my thongs. Pink, did they remind him of her? He'd written that Sandrine liked pink. Was there a special gene for pinkness?

"Is this my father then?" I indicated the man in the photo—a laughing *z'oreille,* a real Frenchman, taut and correct and totally dashing. "What happened to him?"

"Yves-Laurent die in Events as I say in letter."

I placed the photo back. We sat there in silence and I tried to digest what he'd said. I'd been searching for my birth mother for so long I felt cheated that the hunt was over. And how would Namilly feel about it? Or was she too tied up with Alice to care?

"Why'd she do it, Namilly I mean? Like, *take* me?" I whispered.

"Oh, it was Events. I is certain. She run from shooting, run from bombs. She worry for your life." He reached over, and poured me another drink.

"She's probably a Dutch sea wall, they do brave things."

"Dutch sea wall?"

"*Gouine.*" It was the one piece of slang I remembered from my grammar book.

"It matter if she like ze ladies?"

I shook my head. "Not that it's the type of thing you can discuss with your mother. It's just she's so hung up about Alice."

"My country not peaceful even now." Marcel was back in his own little world. "And it is consequence of colonisation."

It seemed I was also a consequence of colonisation.

"I'm like the Orchard Swallowtail," I said, my tongue tripping over the words, "tricked into settling in an alien environment. But, like that butterfly, I survived."

"You will come wis me?" he asked.

Perhaps it wouldn't be so bad to go north, see Sandrine. Would she be rapt? We'd have a fab time together, make up for those lost years. And there was another reason for me to leave.

Jules was homing in.

Chapter 53

"Hi, Mum," I whispered over and over. "*Bonjour, maman. Salut, Sandrine.*" The words sounded weird in French.

Would my birth mother be over the moon to see me? Would she fall to the floor in a faint? It seemed unreal, now it was all happening.

I began to cram clothing into my backpack. I could hear Marcel pacing around the house, stalking from room to room, puffing on a cigarette. He seemed as nervous as I was.

My underwear spilled in all directions. The straps were catching in the zip. Stuff gushed from the tears in the canvas. There was not enough space. I needed Namilly's Louis Vuitton luggage.

I dashed down the passage to the oak armoire. I heaved the door open. A cloud of dust and putridness. I reached for the suitcase. My fingers grasped at nothing. Namilly's suitcase was not there.

Like a maniac, I pushed aside her shoes, raincoats and umbrellas with twisted ribs. Pieces of dried mud scattered about me like biscuit crumbs. The case was definitely not there.

Had Namilly used it herself, left that morning before I woke? Had she found Marcel's letter behind the armoire and fled because of its contents?

I peered into the shadowy gap. No sign of any balled-up paper.

I slid my hand into the slit, pulled against the furniture. The oak skirt grated over the boards, screeched as wood rubbed against wood, until I was able to properly see. I pushed the frizzy fringe from my eyes. But I could make out only the usual accumulation of dust and dead ants, blurred bodies of flying creatures crossed over to the other side.

"She's found your letter, Marcel," I yelled. "It's gone."

No answer. Just a smell of Gauloises Blondes coming from the direction of Namilly's bedroom.

"You're not smoking in there? She'll have your hide," I said, forgetting for a moment I'd not be there to hear her complaints.

"I think she's left, as well," I added. "I think she's nicked off because of those things you told me."

Marcel approached. He seemed distracted.

"What's the matter?"

"Somesing I discover."

I was not interested. I turned and ran, slamming the door behind me. "*Nounou, Nounou,*" I cried.

Through the canna patch, and over the septic tank I went. Leaves slapped. The stench of sewage rose around me. I choked back tears. I called her name. There was only silence.

A mound of lilac branches lay on the ground waiting to be chopped and added to her woodpile. I was free of woodpiles now, of chores. I should be rejoicing. Then how come I didn't feel exhilarated? How come I felt abandoned, when I was the one doing the abandoning? Was it because Namilly'd got there first, trumped me in the get-knotted stakes?

"We 'ave plane to catch." Marcel touched me on the shoulder. "I 'ave somesing to show you before we leave."

I traipsed behind him to Namilly's room. The sheets of her narrow bed were pulled tight. A document lay there, as though forgotten in the rush: a passport with my photo, hair bleached by the sun.

"I told you," I said, pointing to the date of birth. "I'm eighteen in a few months."

"Who is girls?" He held up a photo.

"Beats me. Never seen 'em before."

'Hannah Zimmerman, Prague. Next of kin, Natasha Zimmerman' was scribbled under one.

Marcel pointed. "Portofino it look like." He held up another photo. *'Annabelle Simmons, Ulster—British'* was scrawled on the yellowed paper. *'Next of kin, Millicent Simmons.'*

"I don't know who they are," I said, shrugging. "Anyway, Namilly refuses to fly. She can't have taken those photos."

"Because she SAY she not like to fly? There is more girls before you, I sink."

"Come again."

"All from trouble place. Ireland. Eastern Europe—"

"But it was *me* she saved. She saved *me* from the Events, not them. She saved *me* from the independence war a thousand accords will never fix. We'll never know about them." My voice went crackly. "And now she's gone."

I hefted my ratty backpack, threw it across my shoulder. Loops and lace dangled about me like pieces of my life.

"Natasha, Milly. Join together, make Namilly."

"It's a coincidence that combined they spell her name."

"You were not ze first," he whispered.

"Cool. She had a life before me. I don't care if I was the twenti-eth." I pointed to the hollow sofa. "But I *do* care if there's a hole in that furniture."

Marcel ripped away the padded cover on one end.

"Knothole 'ere." He indicated a fault in the wood. "One zere." He indicated another, and then scratched his chin as if thinking. "Zere was carpenter man who used to make 'em," he said, nodding in the direction of the sofa, "in Magenta, near domestic airport, at time of Events." He chewed his lip thoughtfully. "People buy to use for storage, but I know person who smuggle pedigree dogs to Australia, for avoiding quarantine laws."

Pedigree dogs? Then why not a child? There were knotholes in the wood. I could've breathed, after all.

"Anyway, why you worry about gaps?"

"Gaps?" I murmured, not in the mood to discuss my theory with him. "Well, there's been a mega gap in my memory. And, you know, other mothers shove their kids in cupboards, feed them bits of bread under the crack for days and days. She only did it to me for a short time—put me inside the hollow sofa, I mean." He knew nothing of Namilly's wacky survival techniques.

I locked the door behind me—we had no deadbolts like Win, only one simple lock—and hurried past the simmering cans on the other side of the fence. The flies buzzed and guzzled, creating a purple haze. Marcel's words kept niggling. Had Namilly really cared for other kids? A *nounou* did that. Had she lied to protect me? I was going with him. I would find out.

Chapter 54

Kids screaming. The gentle splash of foam. A swish. The roar of an engine. Fart from an exhaust. The jangle of a mobile phone. Screeching sound of a wiper on glass. Frottage of a cloth. A smoker's cough. The clamminess of the tropics. The sourness of mould. Grit beneath my lids.

I rolled over, adjusted the backpack beneath my head and tried to get back into the dream.

The phone rang again. I prised my lids open. The landline at the unattended Avis desk was ringing. I lurched up. What was I doing here?

I groaned. Of course, I was waiting until someone could identify me so I could fly south. And there'd be other dumps like this, other dummy spitting with people who'd got on with their lives. It would be a long search, probably a fruitless one. But I would soldier on in the search for my identity.

The phone at the desk rang again. The window cleaner on the other side of the glass regarded me with curiosity. How long would I be forced to live in this daggy space, dossed down at the airport? My home a bench? Eating fries from McDonald's? Washing in the ladies loo?

The woman with the Chilean squashed-bug hair was back.

Neanderthal Man in his upright walk socks was back as well. "Like a Kit Kat, girl?" He poked a packet in my face.

"No thanks, I only eat raw vegan."

"I'll get yer a banana then. You're in the right bloody place." He strode off, legs akimbo.

I stretched, hefted my backpack and trailed to the loo.

In the mirror, a desperado eyed me back. I splashed cold water on my face, noticing the frizzy fringe was now straight as a silky terrier's.

I pulled up my T-shirt. In the midst of washing the dirty bits, a woman with a kid—all thongs and shorts and freckled face—came in.

I covered up, and ducked into the dunny. Clamped the seat down, got myself comfortable and began to think. Only one option came to mind, obvious since Sandrine had flicked her hair, adjusted her pareo, and said I wasn't hers.

I jiggled my keys. There was an empty house down south, friends who cared. I could hitchhike, catch a road train, hop on a banana load like Jack Bradfield's green tree frog. And, like it, I would survive.

I left the loo on a mission.

Then I saw him.

Jack Bradfield's photo smiled at me from the front page of the local newspaper, left lying on a bench. Had Jack been arrested for some Peeping Tom activity?

I gobbled up the words: *The eminent Jack Bradfield, an esteemed expert on butterflies in tropical rainforest areas.* I remembered the afternoon in the sandy soil among the ti-trees at Ravella, listening to him talk about his beloved Mountain Blue and its brothers and sisters, and I began to giggle. Boy, Hetty Geiger sure was wacko. Her imagination was more colourful than any butterfly.

I felt proud to have known the great Jack Bradfield.

"Excuse me, mademoiselle," a voice murmured in my ear.

I turned to find the man from the Amédée Apartments.

Marcel was there, too, chatting up the bird with the cochinealed hair. He interrupted his conversation, pressed the button of his mobile phone.

"What gives? Am I being let go at last, put on the plane back home with the two of you to see me off?"

"Claude Ponsinet." He held out his hand. "Can we talk?"

I followed this mountain of a man. He had the biggest 'fro I'd ever seen. His legs were huge. His floral shirt billowed as he led me to my plastic perch.

"What gives?" I asked again.

"She not want see you no more." His words were careful. "*Jamais encore*. Never again."

"Who? Sandrine?" I blinked.

The Kanak nodded. His eyes were kind.

"But I'm not, like, her daughter. Why would I bother to fizz her off? I was *not stalking or anything*."

"She not sleep ever, after you come."

"You mean it kept her awake for a night? You mean *she* lost sleep because *I* turned up?" I fiddled with my French plait. "Well, I've lost a lifetime of sleep wondering."

"You no understand. She much tired," he whispered.

"Are you saying the DNA was ridgy-didge?" I wiped my clammy hands on my jeans.

His eyes slid away from mine.

So, he hadn't denied the results of those tests.

"You mean she's too fatigued to speak to her own *daughter*?" My mouth went rubbery. The words felt like cotton wool.

"You no understand." He shook his head. "She no say zat. She say you must stay away, zat is all."

I lifted my hands in a defensive gesture. "Okay, I'll stay away. Heaven *forbid* I should cause her to lose another night's sleep." My throat went rigid. "She took snaps for Papa of someone else's daughter. Yet she's not interested in finding her *own*. What a loser!"

The spicy man stayed mute.

"Doesn't she love her daughter, want to know her?"

"Love is illusion." He gave a shrug, and I understood why Namilly felt so bitter.

Monsieur Ponsinet pushed himself up. He held out his hand again but I turned my head away. He padded off, and I could see why Sandrine had given up everything for this man. But I refused to give up on her. I would find some way to make her talk to me.

Marcel drifted in my direction, still talking on his mobile phone. His shades clung to his forehead. He was not wearing his navy-blue boat shoes that day. His thongs were new.

"I fix ticket. You will be home soon." He pointed at the check-in chick who gave me a tight smile.

"Thanks for not leaving me in the lurch," I said.

"Is for you." He offered me the cell phone.

My heart beat fast. Sandrine?

"It is your *copain*." Marcel's smile was grave.

"Stefan?" I was in a solid gold nightmare of my very own making.

"Zere is tragedy."

"Stef?" I pressed the phone against my ear. "What's wrong?"

"Alice Winstone's dead," he said.

"I know she's ill." My voice jiggled in my throat. "But she's not that old."

"Electrocution, mate."

"Come again. She was electrocuted?" I stiffened. "How?"

"Pissed on Win's hairdryer."

"You mean the hairdryer fell into the bath?"

"No, mate. She turned on the hairdryer, pissed upon it."

I could feel hysteria bubble up inside me. Surely Stefan was having me on? Silence at the other end. I knew he was serious.

"But it must've been an accident."

"Fair dinks."

"Was Win with her when it happened?" My chest tightened at the thought of Win being hauled off again in the divvy van.

"Your mother was with her." His voice was faint.

"I thought Namilly'd skedaddled."

"Nope. Rolled up at the Winstone house that morning, suitcase packed, ready for the long haul."

"Why are *you* telling me this? Why are *you* in the equation?"

"Pulled your ma out of The Cauldron, mate. She tried to do herself in after. First thing she said was, 'If I die, tell Genna I smuggled her …'."

His voice crackled, disappeared for a second, surged back. "Something about that hollow sofa you're always on about. Your old lady needs you."

Namilly needed *me*? I was glad. I needed to be needed.

"Anyway, what're you doing all the way up there?"

"Oh, I think I found my birth mother." The words came out in a sort of sob.

Silence at the other end. More crackling.

"She doesn't want to see me." My voice caught. "But I'll find a way."

Stefan's words were breaking up, coming and going.

The reverse thrust of an engine. Tree ferns trembled, bent double from the blast of the avtur.

A clearing of throat the other end. A growl. A mumble. "Well, *I* want to see you."

Had Stefan *really* said that? His voice came through again, as if he were standing right next to me.

"There's a sleaze asked about you. Gold hoop earring in his ear, big one."

"Did he give his name?"

"Called himself Elise, but he's a bloke. Geezer over thirty, dyed hair."

Uh-oh, that description fitted Jules. Served me right for using chat rooms. "I'll explain, um, when I see you."

"What's that about, mate?" Stefan sounded jealous.

www.ingramcontent.com/pod-product-compliance
Lightning Source LLC
Chambersburg PA
CBHW070601130626
46556CB00001B/232